CERIDWEN DOVEY
Only the Animals

Atlantic Books
London

Published in E-book and paperback in Great Britain in 2015
by Atlantic Books, an imprint of Atlantic Books Ltd.

First published in Australia in 2014 by Penguin Group.

Text copyright © Ceridwen Dovey, 2014

Illustrations copyright © Teresa Dovey, 2014

10 9 8 7 6 5 4 3 2 1

A CIP catalogue record for this book is available from the British Library.

Paperback ISBN: 978 1 78239 717 5
E-book ISBN: 978 1 78239 718 2

Typeset in 11.5/17.5 Adobe Caslon
Printed and bound by CPI Group (UK) Ltd, Croydon, CR0 4YY

Atlantic Books
An Imprint of Atlantic Books Ltd
Ormond House
26–27 Boswell Street
London
WC1N 3JZ

www.atlantic-books.co.uk

Ceridwen Dovey's debut novel, *Blood Kin*, was published in fifteen countries, shortlisted for the Dylan Thomas Prize, and selected for the US National Book Foundation's prestigious "5 Under 35" honours list. She studied social anthropology at Harvard and New York University, and now lives with her husband and son in Sydney. *Only the Animals* won the 2014 Readings New Australian Writing Award and the Queensland Premier's Literary Awards Steele Rudd Award for a short story collection.

ALSO BY CERIDWEN DOVEY

Blood Kin

On one side there is luminosity, trust, faith, the beauty of the earth; on the other side, darkness, doubt, unbelief, the cruelty of the earth, the capacity of people to do evil. When I write, the first side is true; when I do not the second is.

Czesław Miłosz, ROAD-SIDE DOG

Each creature is key to all other creatures. A dog sitting in a patch of sun licking itself, says he, is at one moment a dog and at the next a vessel of revelation.

J.M. Coetzee, ELIZABETH COSTELLO

For Gethin and Chiara

CONTENTS

THE
BONES

Soul of Camel

Died 1892, Australia

The three of us were nodding off around the campfire, the queen's yellow bones in a sack beside my owner, when I saw the goanna watching us again, the same one that had stalked us through the bush for days.

Mister Mitchell was already asleep on his swag, wrapped in an expensive blanket he had brought with him from Sydney for the expedition. But the poet drifter we'd picked up in Hungerford, Henry Lawson, was still awake. He lifted the square of calico he'd put over his eyes to block out the light of the moon and listened. The goanna was moving through the dry leaves, making them scrape against one another like cartilage.

It was summer in the back country, the night of Christmas. The men had eaten too much dinner – doughboys fried over the fire, boggabri to pass as greens, salted mutton that Henry Lawson had cadged from one of the sheep stations we'd passed along the track. And we had all had too much rum.

'I told Mitchell to put the bones back,' Henry Lawson said. 'I warned him. Since we were boys together, he's been stubborn. He was born on the Grenfell goldfields, like me, you know. Hadn't seen him in years 'til he walked into the pub in Hungerford. His father got lucky, got rich. Mine didn't. They moved out, disappeared to Sydney.'

I waited. In the short time we had spent together, I'd learned that when Henry Lawson was dehydrated or drunk – and he was usually one or the other – he talked to himself out loud.

'He'll go to hell for it, he will,' Henry Lawson said. 'The goanna's come to take him there. The ghost of Christmas past.' He gave a laugh, but his eyes, almost as big and liquid as my own, were watchful. The goanna had spooked him. It certainly spooked me. It was huge, more like a crocodile than a lizard, with frightening claws.

'My mother used to read me Dickens as a boy, if you can believe it,' he said. 'We lived in a tent with a bark room out front, lined with newspapers, a door made of glass left behind in the last goldrush, a whitewashed floor. But still she read me Dickens, and Poe. I can hardly believe it myself.'

Was he in fact talking to me? It was unclear. Not since my handler, Zeriph, passed away years before in Bourke had a human spoken to me casually, for the sake of conversation. Mostly all I got was *'Hoosh!'* and *'Itna!'* Down. Up. Up. Down. I lowed quietly in response, as encouragement, and settled more comfortably onto my thick kneepads on the sand. The rum had made me thirsty, but I knew the waterbags Mister Mitchell had filled with tank water in Hungerford were almost empty and it was no use begging for more.

Hungerford. Of all the strange, half-formed places I'd seen since I was brought here, it was one of the strangest, straddling the border between Queensland and New South Wales, a rabbit-proof fence down the main street, a couple of houses on one side, five on the other. After sampling a few glasses of sour yeast at one of the two pubs (both on the Queensland side), Henry Lawson joked the town should instead have been called Hungerthirst. Then he pointed out with a twinkle in his eye that there were rabbits on either side of the fence.

'That was back in Pipeclay, where our fathers were fossicking on the goldfields,' Henry Lawson said, laying the calico square over his eyes again. 'Most of the other diggers had left by then. Their holes had collapsed, their huts were haunted. The first ghost I ever saw came at me from one of those huts, the ghost of a Chinese digger murdered for bottoming on too much payable gold. He used to sit up in the forked trunk of the blue gum above our tent, making the branches sway even on nights when there was no wind.'

I too have ghosts in my past, I wanted to tell Henry Lawson. The ghosts of the other camels who were shipped with me from our birthplace on the island of Tenerife, sold along with our handlers – who had come from somewhere else far away – to an Englishman on his way to Australia. I was the only one of my caravan to survive that dreadful sea journey. The women died around me in the hold, one by one.

And the ghost of the bachelor camel I killed near Alice Springs, who challenged me by grinding his teeth together. I suffocated him, squashed his head between my leg and body, though there were no females around to compete over and we should instead have become friends. Zeriph never let me forget my stupidity, killing that bull. He felt sorry for the other handler, who grieved over his dead camel as if for a child.

'Our schoolhouse – the one Mitchell and I went to as boys – was haunted,' Henry Lawson said, sitting up to suck the last drops from his black bottle of rum. 'By the bushranger Ben Hall's ghost. The troopers had murdered him in his sleep out on the Lachlan Plain. We thought he was a hero of the people. Mother said he was a common thief. Funny thing was, my little brother couldn't decide if he wanted to be a bushranger or a trooper when he grew up. That was the choice for us boys from the bush – outlaw or agent of the law! Ha!'

He lay back down on his swag, leaving his face uncovered. Slowly he raised one arm and pointed a long accusatory finger at the moon. 'At Sunday School we were told it was wicked to point at the moon.' The rum had stopped his shakes. 'And we were told our blacks are the lowest race on earth. There was a painting of some Aborigines hung on the schoolroom wall, but they looked more like you, like camels, peculiar creatures that shouldn't exist, than like the black men we knew.'

But I do exist, I thought. I may have oval red blood cells, three stomach compartments, and urine as thick as syrup, but I exist. I watched him, still pointing at the moon. I felt sick, not just from the rum. Homesick.

'A black man's ghost turned up at one of my mother's séances,' he went on. 'She had joined the local Spiritualist Society – it was the thing to do in the bush for a while – and she let me come along to one of the meetings. A lot of teamsters had joined, and the first hour of the séance was taken up by them asking the medium to check whether any of the spirits might know the location of their missing bullocks.'

He chuckled, and shook his head hard as if to clear it. 'Mitchell's father was at that meeting. His wife didn't know he was there. He had come to ask the spirits for help finding gold, but the medium couldn't answer those questions. Then a different spirit came knocking. It wanted to speak to Mitchell's father through the medium. "Who are you?" she kept asking, but it wouldn't say. "Have you met in spirit land many you knew on earth?" the medium asked. "Yes," was the reply.'

Henry Lawson lowered his voice. 'Then the medium said, out of nowhere, "Hospital Creek. Do you know of it?" Mitchell's father's sunburned face went pale. "Yes," he said. "I worked at the stock-yard there." The medium was silent for a long time. "I'm getting – a fire. A fire of some kind." Mitchell's father said nothing. "Bodies in a fire," she said. "A lot of them." And at this, Mitchell's father began to shake, a grown man trembling, but not with fear. With rage. "You bitch," he spat, "don't you know how to keep your mouth shut like the rest of us?"'

Henry Lawson threw the empty bottle of rum out into the bush, in the direction of the goanna. The goanna didn't move, didn't even flinch. 'So the séance ended, and soon afterwards Mitchell's father struck gold,' he said.

I thought of the place Mister Mitchell had taken me, where he dug in the earth for the queen's bones. Had it been near a creek? Perhaps, though it was hard to tell; it was the time of year when most of the creek beds were dry. I had been distracted by the goanna from the beginning. It had appeared as Mitchell brushed soil from the bones, clinging with its claws to the carved tree to which I was tethered beside the grave.

My mouth felt dry, and I was gripped by the urge to spit up some of my regurgitated cud, something that Zeriph had almost managed to train out of me, except when I was very angry or upset. Or drunk, I thought with shame. The green fluid landed heavily in the fire, and sizzled a bit as it burned.

Henry Lawson found this amusing. 'Now that will go very well with the last spittle I encountered, in Hungerford.' He dug around under his swag for his notebook, paged through, and began to read aloud. 'After tea had a yarn with an old man who was mind-ing a mixed flock of goats and sheep; and we asked him whether he thought Queensland was better than New South Wales, or the other way about. He scratched the back of his head, and thought awhile . . . at last, with the bored air of a man who has gone through the same performance too often before, he stepped deliberately up to the fence and spat over it into New South Wales. After which he got leisurely through and spat back on Queensland. "That's what *I* think of the blanky colonies!" he said.'

Henry Lawson laughed. He looked cross-eyed and vulnerable from the rum. His gaze slipped onto the goanna at the outer rim of firelight, its loose, scaled throat illuminated.

It wasn't a childhood bond or the rum keeping Henry Lawson by our campfire night after night. He'd told Mister Mitchell that if it were shearing season he would have stopped off to work on the stations and let us be on our way back to Bourke with the bones without him. But he was lying. We were the perfect quarry for a writer sent out to dig around in the bush for copy, almost too good to be true: a madman collector on a camel, son of a man who'd made the family fortune on the goldfields, carrying the stolen bones of an Aboriginal queen from long ago, all while being stalked by a giant goanna. I'd heard him say he liked to put animals in his stories because it made the humans look worse.

'They didn't really have queens,' was the first thing Henry Lawson said after listening to Mister Mitchell's explanation for what he was doing riding a camel along the stock route in midsummer. It wasn't unusual to see an entire caravan of camels lugging supplies across the vast desert, especially further north (we had been brought to this country for that purpose; a railroad was being built on our backs), but as a lone camel, used by Mister Mitchell rather like a fancy horse, I became part of his oddity. 'Not in the way we think of a queen.'

'The queen's bones,' Mister Mitchell had repeated in his dreamy way, and Henry Lawson had let it go.

The first day of our journey, the day after Mister Mitchell had bought me in Bourke, he decided it was too hot to wear his boots, and burned his feet to blistering in the noon sun while murmuring to himself the instructions he'd been given on how to ride a camel. 'Keep your hands by your sides, relax, and sway with the creature as best you can.'

I became afraid then that he would get us lost, and bit a hole in one of the bags of flour hanging against my flanks, to leave a trail. That only worked as long as we had flour, and soon we didn't, and the white trail on the red sand ended abruptly. I cursed myself then for not taking the chance to run away after Zeriph died, off into the redder centre to join the ranks of wild camels whose numbers were rumoured to be swelling, desert outlaws who spent their days destroying the very same things they had lugged to the interior in the first place: stock fences, well casings, railroad tracks, water pumps.

The goanna scuttled closer to the fire, jerking its flat head, then it froze and was once more unsettlingly still. I felt my long spine tingle.

'They eat meat,' Henry Lawson said. 'All kinds of meat. Fresh or rotting. I've heard they'll eat the eyes out of a sleeping man's face, or drag a whole sheep off in their jaws. I saw one kill a kangaroo and take chunks of flesh out of it like a dingo. One bite, they say, and you never stop bleeding.'

I looked at Mister Mitchell's padded, sleeping form. He had the bag of bones beside him, clutching it to him like a lover. The way he was lying – on his side, his knees pulled up and head tucked in – reminded me of the way the queen's bones had been arranged in her mounded grave. She had not been laid out on her back when she was buried, arms straight, legs out straight. She had been laid into the earth carefully curled up on her side.

'His father was fixated on those bones,' Henry Lawson muttered. 'Like father, like son. They've both always been a bit touched.' He snapped his head around to look at me, as if I had said something. 'Oh no, it's not what you think. These aren't *those* bones. Not from the killings at Hospital Creek. They made sure to burn those ones up, get rid of the evidence. The queen – he does insist on calling her that, doesn't he? – is from a time before we were here, before old Captain Cook even. Someone at the stockyard told his father about the queen's grave. Now he thinks if he has her bones, the Hospital Creek ghosts will let him alone.'

The goanna hissed, inflating flaps of skin around its throat into a menacing neckpiece.

Henry Lawson ignored it and began to sing softly. 'We three kings of Orient are/bearing gifts we traverse afar . . . My god, I'm thirsty. Imagine dying of thirst. You hear about Ebenezer Davis, who was taking a mob of Kerribree sheep along the stock route and got lost? They found his body last week beside an empty waterbag and a note. The sheep had buggered off and left him. Hold on,' he said, and turned the pages of his notebook again. 'Ah, yes. Good man. I did write it down. "My Tung is stkig to my mouth and I see what I have wrote I know it is this is the last time I may have of expressing feeling alive and the feeling exu is lost for want of water My ey Dassels. My tong burn. I can see no More God Help."' Henry Lawson sighed. 'I must find a way to use this. Great theme, death in the bush. Death in general. My ey Dassels. My tong burn.'

I decided then and there that in the morning, once I'd slept off the rum, I was going to run away from Mister Mitchell and Henry Lawson, and gallop on my spindly legs until I was deep enough into the desert to forget what I could not understand. None of it made any sense: Hospital Creek, the ghosts on the goldfields, the bonfire, the queen's bones, the goanna. I wasn't blameless, but I was innocent of *this*, of whatever Henry Lawson and Mister Mitchell and their kind had done. I had only arrived a few years ago, how could I have done anything wrong?

'God, Bourke. Of all places to ring in the New Year,' Henry Lawson was saying, picking his teeth. 'We'll be back by then, I suppose. Let's see. There's still Youngerina Bore, Fords Bridge, Sutherlands Lake, Walkdens Bore. Then Bourke. It'll be too hot to think or write. Too hot to do anything but drink until you feel about life as you ought to feel before you start. You know what they say about people who die in Bourke? They get to hell and find it chilly, and send back for their blankets.' He laughed. 'Many's the night I've lain in the dust outside the Carriers Arms, listening to the drunks making jokes about the Salvation Army woman who sings hymns outside the hotel, all day, all night. It doesn't matter if a woman's cracked, they say, s'long as the crack's in the right place.'

Mister Mitchell suddenly rolled onto his back, threw off the blanket and jumped to his feet, facing the goanna where it stood watching, still as quartz, a few feet away from him. He was sweating. 'Father warned me about you,' Mister Mitchell said, swaying, pointing at the goanna. 'He said to kill you, drain off your oil, eat your flesh, and burn your bones to ashes. It's you he dreams about, you who comes to haunt him. It's you who saw him light the bonfire.'

'You've nothing but the jim-jams, Mitchell, you've drunk too much rum,' Henry Lawson said. 'Lie down, go back to sleep. It's Christmas night, for God's sake. Ignore the animals. They're our only and most loyal spectators.'

Mister Mitchell ignored him instead. He dug around in his supplies for his shot belt, and began to load slugs in one barrel of his muzzle-loader and ball in another. Henry Lawson didn't stop his old friend. His eyes had glazed over – the rum, yes, but I could tell something else had gripped him. He had to see how it all ended.

Mister Mitchell tamped down the wadding with the ramrod and lifted his gun, aiming at the goanna. 'The bones are *mine*!'

The goanna bolted in my direction. I lunged to my feet. There was an excruciating silence.

The goanna was dead, I saw that first. I felt my cheek against the cold midnight sand, and found myself thinking of a moment years before, when Zeriph had loosened the ropes and I was finally relieved of the terrible weight of the upright piano I'd carried on my back, all the way from the railhead at Oodnadatta to Alice Springs, counterbalanced by a drum of water.

Zeriph had been proud of me, carrying the first piano into the core of our new country. Not copper from the mines, not wool wagons to the mills, not reckless explorers, not railroad tracks nor overland telegraph supplies, not one of the mounted Oodnadatta policemen on patrol. A piano. A thing of beauty.

But for what? I carried that thing of beauty all that way on my back, with the ropes cutting into my bones, so that somebody could tinkle on the keys for the midday drunks at the pub in Alice. That's what broke Zeriph's heart, that the piano's music could mean nothing without the false prophetry of drink.

I tried to move my head so that I was facing Mecca, but I became confused. I thought I saw a figure in the bush. For a moment I believed the goanna had transformed itself into a woman, into the queen herself. Then I realised the figure was Henry Lawson, half hidden behind a tree, laughing hysterically at the scene before him: a dead goanna, a dying camel, a white man clutching a bag of old bones.

'I've got it!' he said, between gasps. 'I've got the last line . . . And the sun rose again on the grand Australian bush – the nurse and tutor of eccentric minds, the home of the weird. I've got it!'

My ey Dassels. My tong burn. Oh, Mister Lawson, be careful. You're not the only one who can tell a good story about death in the wastelands.

PIGEONS,
A PONY,
THE TOMCAT
AND I

Soul of Cat

Died 1915, France

*O crossing of looks! Bond that the animal tries to tighten
and that man always undoes!*

Sidonie-Gabrielle Colette,
LOOKING BACKWARDS: RECOLLECTIONS

Waiting for the tomcat

It is long after midnight and still the tomcat has not returned to
his parapet above the trench adjacent to mine. I have been waiting
for him, primed by the soldiers' talk of his legendary night-hunting
skills out in no man's land and the way he fearlessly cleans himself while exposed in the sun on the parapet, even in the heaviest
bombardments. The soldiers welcomed me when I arrived but
seemed a little disappointed that I wasn't also a tom – they like to
bet on anything and everything, these boys, and I think they would
have liked a wager on who would win the scrap of the tomcats.

What they don't know is that I've always felt I was meant to be a tom and not a she-cat. Colette understands this, my beloved Colette who inadvertently left me behind here at the front after a brave secret visit to her new husband, the awful Henri, who was made sergeant at the outbreak of war and fully believes he deserves the title. She didn't know that I'd stowed away in her vehicle in Paris, overcoming my detestation of blur and movement. But while I was outside the car, distracted by a blackbird, she was discovered and sent back to Paris, before I'd been able to surprise her with the warmth of my body at her shins. Now I'm trapped here until she realises what has happened – she will, I'm sure of it, with her cat-like instincts – and returns to collect me.

I've kept a low profile, and done my surveillance work discreetly. The officers' quarters, far from the fire trenches, appealed due to their trimmings and comforts, but I know the sergeant has always been jealous of Colette's love for me, and would be delighted to see me harmed. Alone with him one evening in their apartment in Paris, I sensed his malevolence so strongly that my usually dry paws became wet with sweat, and I disappeared the way only a cat can and did not re-emerge from my hiding place until she was home.

I moved away from the base reserve camp, past the support line, and arrived at this mud-churned front, though I would dearly have loved to stay close to the pigeon loft to catch one of those earnest little birds ferrying messages in aluminium capsules attached to their legs. Can it be true they are motivated to fly the distances they do for the meagre promise of being reunited with their mate on the other side of the partition on their return? They look delicious to me even when they come back ragged and bloody, almost torn apart by German bullets or German hawks, about to drop dead from fatigue. I enjoyed the jokes their human handlers told too. A male pigeon falls in love with a female pigeon and sets up a rendezvous at the top of the Eiffel Tower. He arrives on time. Two hours later, when he is about to give up and leave, she arrives and says casually, 'So sorry I'm late. It's such a lovely day, I thought I'd walk.'

The fire trench is not my ideal environment, but at least I know the sergeant will rarely set foot here, and the young men who fill these trenches are so miserably bothered by rats which have developed a taste for human flesh that they are glad to claim me as their own trench cat to rival the tomcat next door. It shocked Colette to see what has become of this swathe of the countryside. So many times I have accompanied her on visits to her mother in the small village in Burgundy where she grew up in pastoral paradise. She can summon vignettes of a way of life that most Parisians have long lost: resting her feet on a metal foot warmer filled with embers in a cold schoolroom; feasting on sloes from the hedges and on haws; the chestnut skins she'd throw in the fire, to her mother's chagrin, for they'd later spoil the ash lye spread over the bucking cloth on the laundry tub, and stain the linen. Autumn was always her favourite season, and it became mine too once I had seen Burgundy. It was just as she'd promised: the last peaches, the triangular beechnuts, and the red leaves of the cherry trees quivering in the November dawn.

But this late autumn at the front is unlike any I have witnessed. Without the changing palette of the trees to signal the shift towards winter (the leaves have been exploded off), and the songbirds mostly gone quiet, it becomes difficult to know where I am, in what season, in which century. Between my trench and the foremost trenches of the Germans, there is no living thing except rats anymore. Instead there is an ocean of mud, liquid enough that when the wind blows it forms ripples on the surface of the largest shell craters; pools deep enough to drown a man. Paris and its millennial amusements must have been a mirage, for how could that have led to this?

Neighbours

The tom returned when the sun was eking out a cold light. The soldiers had just stood down from their dawn stand-to-arms on the firestep, shooting off their 'morning hate', as the ritual of firing into the early mists – the Germans do the same – is called. Worn out from anticipating the tom's return in the night, I was no longer prepared, half dozing on my own parapet. The soldiers were wrapping and rewrapping their rotting feet before gingerly fitting on their boots. They had cleaned their rifles, and the senior officers had inspected them, and it was time for the breakfast truce, during which each side (on good days) let the other eat in peace.

One of the soldiers – very thin, very young – offered me some of his condensed-milk ration, and I stuck my nose up at it in worst pussycat fashion because I couldn't bear to take from him his small chance at nourishment. But he looked so dismayed that I climbed down, lapped it up, and thanked him with a guttural purr and a nudge of my head against his legs.

It was then that the tomcat's outline appeared against the grey sky and I knew I'd lost my chance to surprise him in a show of dominance. I would have to change tactics.

'Careful, little one,' the soldier whispered, looking up. 'You've got company.'

As nonchalantly as I could, I climbed back up the side of the trench and out onto the parapet. Some of the other soldiers stopped their morning task of repairing duckboards to watch, whistling and joking about a love match between two cats equally dimwitted enough to expose themselves to German snipers in daylight.

The tomcat looked at me. 'Kiki?' he said. 'Kiki-la-Doucette?'

I didn't recognise him. I said nothing, licking my paws.

'It's really you, isn't it?' he said. 'I don't believe this. I'm sharing a trench with the famous Kiki-la-Doucette!'

'I'm giving you fifteen seconds to clear out,' I said. 'Fifteen, fourteen, thirteen —'

'You don't remember me? I live down the road from you in Paris. My owner started walking me on a leash after she saw Colette walking you, to my great embarrassment. We came once to your apartment for a salon of sorts, and I'll never forget my first sight of Missy, wearing that tuxedo adjusted to fit her womanly shape. There was a strange musician playing otherworldly notes on the piano, someone called Ravel. Colette's bulldog took an instant dislike to me, so we didn't stay long, but you and I shared a bowl of milk and I was so awed by being in your presence that I couldn't say a word.'

'Twelve, eleven, ten —' I kept up my count rather brutally, for I did remember, suddenly, that shared bowl of milk.

'My owner was in love with Colette, you see. She always watched for her at the window, and read her newspaper columns out loud to me, or the nasty reviews of her latest music-hall performance – there was one where she took on the persona of a cat, I remember, with whiskers and a black nose.'

I was overwhelmed with such longing that I forgot to keep my countdown going. She'd developed her mime for the title role in *The Loved-up Cat* at Le Bataclan by observing me even more closely than usual, crawling around on the floor after me, copying my every move and twitch and affectation. She didn't have to try very hard to be catty; her young friend Jean Cocteau has the knack of seeing through her niceties and he likes to warn new acquaintances, whoever is her friend du jour: 'Her velvet paw shows its claws very fast. And when she scratches, she leaves a gash.' They usually don't believe him until it's too late, until they are bleeding.

Toby-Chien the bulldog didn't mind all the attention Colette paid me. He was used to playing second fiddle; it was always clear that in her hierarchy of loves, cats came above dogs, and any four-legged creature came above those of the two-legged variety, even dear Missy. You wouldn't think it, but I could always count on Toby-Chien for a good chat when I felt like one. Colette would observe us wryly from the kitchen table with her cigarette poised, and that's where she got the idea for her Animals in Dialogue columns which she published in *La Vie Parisienne*, imagining what Toby-Chien and I were talking about, though in that she was often wrong. We didn't care much about the scandal of her open-mouthed kiss with Missy – whose stage name was Yssim – on the stage at the Moulin Rouge, and we'd never liked her ex-husband Willy, and once he was gone from our lives we didn't talk much about him. But these were the things she knew that Paris was preoccupied with, and Colette, just finding her feet as a stage presence and an author, never missed an opportunity to give Paris what it desired.

'My owner hated Missy with a passion,' the tomcat was saying. 'Called her mutton dressed up as lamb, though it wasn't her age that Missy was trying to disguise. She thought Missy looked ridiculous in those baggy men's clothes with that thin moustache pencilled above her top lip. My owner believed she could give

Colette what she really wanted, a woman's gentle love, unsullied by any pretence at masculinity; a mother and lover all in one. Isn't that what Colette is searching for, somebody to love her as consumingly as her mother?'

I thought of our apartment on the rue de Villejust, where she and Toby-Chien and I lived after her divorce from Willy, until she got married again, to the despicable Henri. Missy lived half a block away in an apartment where she turned out bathroom fixtures on a lathe and held Sapphic salons for ladies who came dressed as men and stood around drinking expensive wine and smoking cigars. Missy made a pair of moustaches from hair plucked from her poodle's tail for herself and Colette, and sometimes they wore matching pince-nez, white trousers, black jackets made from alpaca wool, and several pairs of socks to fill up men's shoes. A regular game for members of the salon, initiated by Colette, was to think up imaginary titles of books that one of the women who worked at the Bibliothèque nationale would make sure afterwards to insert surreptitiously into the official catalogue. The ones Colette came up with usually had me in mind; my favourite was *Diary of a Pussy in Mourning: Kiki-la-Doucette on Breaking Her Long Animal Silence.*

The soldiers in the trench beneath had lost interest and turned back to their tasks. I felt I owed it to them to enliven their morning, and the tomcat's knowledge of intimate details of Colette and Missy's life together had made me angry. Without warning, I leapt forward and hissed at him, swiping at his face with one of my paws and grazing his nose. The soldiers looked up, and laughed.

The tomcat backed off and stared at me forlornly. 'Why did you do that, Kiki?'

'Because I felt like it,' I said. 'If you knew anything about her, you'd know that she and Missy are no longer together. She's remarried now. Her mother is dead. And Colette has her very own baby daughter, Bel-Gazou. Now piss off.'

To my surprise, he did, disappearing into his trench, forgoing the weak sunlight.

I have been lying up here on the parapet and moping since then, trying, and mostly succeeding, to ignore the whine and thunder of the shells the Germans send occasionally across the mud towards us. I pine for Colette and, the truth is, I miss Missy. The tomcat is right. I always knew Colette would leave her eventually. Why she then picked the sergeant, who is drawn to the masculine space of politics and warmongering in an increasingly exclusionary manner, I don't understand. But Colette is not always transparent to me emotionally, just as my needs are sometimes opaque to her.

Fufu and the egg

After a massive artillery barrage aimed at the enemy's front line, the order was given late this afternoon for the men to go over the top in another futile attempt at inching forward our position. I couldn't watch. The thin soldier who believes himself my adopted owner gave me a squeeze before he climbed out obediently and began to wade through the mud, his rifle lifted with the bayonet pointing ahead as if it might give him some sort of magic protection against bullets and shells.

I left the empty trench and staying hidden retreated to the base field hospital and division kitchen, set up in relative safety far behind the front line. The medical orderlies were waiting for the action to end so that they could retrieve bodies, but for now there was little they could do. To distract themselves, one had hidden an egg from an old pony they call Fufu, who drags stretchers piled with the wounded. I watched as Fufu wavered between two dominant preoccupations: finding the egg, and lying down with her forelegs outstretched and eyes closed every time she heard the wail of an incoming shell. As soon as it had exploded at a distance, up she'd get, ready to keep searching for the egg.

'Fufu!' The tomcat had followed me and was calling out to the pony. 'Fufu, over here!'

I looked sideways at the tomcat, with a glance I tried to fill with disdain.

Fufu came towards us. 'Did you see where they hid the egg?' she said.

'It's under the side flap of the tent,' the tomcat said.

'Thanks,' she said. 'Who's this?'

'This,' the tomcat said proudly, 'is Kiki-la-Doucette, who belongs to one of Paris's most fascinating denizens, the theatre performer and author Colette. Many consider Kiki to be Colette's true muse.'

Fufu looked at me with interest. 'Welcome to the front,' she said. 'Did Colette put you out on the streets when war was declared, like this one's owner did?'

The tomcat looked ashamed.

'Of course not,' I said. 'She would never do that. I was left behind here accidentally when she made a secret visit to her husband. And you?'

'Fufu's owners fought hard to keep her,' the tomcat said. 'They even wrote a letter to the commander-in-chief asking for her to be spared being called up.'

'Dear Sir,' Fufu recited, a faraway look in her eyes. 'We are writing for our pony, who we are very afraid may be taken for the army. Please spare her. She is seventeen years old. It would break our hearts to let her go. We have given two other ponies, and our three older brothers are now fighting for France. Maman says she will do anything for the war effort but please let us keep old Fufu, and send official word *quickly* before anyone comes to take her away. Your little patriots, Marie and Claude.'

Another distant shell announced its incoming trajectory and Fufu promptly lay down and closed her eyes. When it had exploded somewhere in the mudlands, she stood up again. 'The letter didn't work,' she said. 'They took me anyway. Now if you'll excuse me, I'm going to go and eat my egg.'

The tomcat looked at me nervously. 'Would you like to come hunting with me tonight?' he said.

'No,' I said. 'I'd like you to leave me alone.'

He slunk off in the direction of the trenches and I felt briefly sorry for him, abandoned by his owner, until I caught sight of a red-breasted robin stunned into silence by the bombardment. The bird was perched on a branch of a leafless apple tree that should have been glowing in full autumn glory, and I decided to terrorise the beautiful creature for a while.

Dumb animals

Colette and I have always been interested in mules, perhaps because we consider ourselves hybrids of a sort, never quite able to fit within the boundaries of our sex or species, always feeling we've a smudgy, mongrel character. It's this very quality in mules that makes them so appealing. They get their vigour from being half horse, half donkey; they are courageous and full of stamina. And of course she and I identify with the refusal of mules to be anything they don't truly feel themselves to be. Humans tend to call this bad manners or lack of respect for authority, but I call it the highest form of authenticity.

So I was gladdened by the sight of a pack of mules bringing around fresh rations for the soldiers in the trenches after sunset, the food loaded into panniers on their backs. Until I tried to talk to one of them and he couldn't answer me except with an awful whispering noise.

The tomcat materialised beside me, obeying the rules of what Colette calls Cat Law, the ability to appear in a place where, a moment before, we have not been.

'They give away our position with their braying if their vocal chords aren't cut,' he said. 'These mules will have travelled a long way carrying supplies to the base camp. And tomorrow they'll probably be put to work carrying munitions.'

I looked more closely at the man driving the mules. He was far too old to fight. The mules showed none of their usual inclination to misbehave and were following him peaceably. 'They love him,' I said.

'And he them. I've seen a driver refuse to leave his team of battery mules when they became entangled in barbed wire. He died with them.'

'Why are so many of them missing their tails?' I asked.

'When they're starving, they eat each other's tails.'

'Colette would adopt them all,' I said. 'On the spot. She'd take them back to Paris to live with us in the apartment. She kept an adopted baby tiger for a while, until it grew too big.'

A mule at the back of the pack had spotted a uniformed sergeant among the soldiers and promptly took a big toothy swipe at his backside. By the time the man had turned around to spot the culprit, the mule was innocently trudging forward and the sergeant could not accuse him without losing his dignity.

'He probably did that just for our benefit,' the tomcat said, 'to remind us he is more than an object of pity.'

My skinny soldier brought over scraps from his meal for me and the tom.

'Don't eat any of it,' I said.

The tomcat looked offended at my suggesting he would take the food. 'I have my own adopted soldier. But you should eat what he's offering even if you're not hungry. You might be the only thing keeping him alive until he's rotated out of the front line and can get some rest.'

I looked up at the young man. He'd been hurt in the advance, not badly, but his shoulder was bandaged. He has made a friend among the other soldiers, who helps him bind his feet and dress his wounds and who sleeps close beside him in the cold nights. I do my best to cement their friendship by enduring the other boy's well-meaning but suffocating hugs. He must only have owned dogs in his life, for he has no idea of the subtleties of what cats like, of our necessary distance.

Glowing in the dark

'Come on,' the tomcat said to me once all the soldiers except the night sentries were asleep. 'I want to show you something.'

I was enjoying myself on the parapet, having tormented a rat for a while by letting it think it was about to escape and pawing it back, and finally eaten it. 'I'm too full to move,' I said. 'Almost too full to talk.'

He turned to go and I felt bad, and lonely. 'I'm coming,' I said, dragging myself up and stretching out my forelegs.

'Good,' he said. 'You won't be sorry, Kiki, I promise.'

'As long as you know nothing's going to happen between us,' I said archly. 'I'm not really a fan of toms in general.'

'I know,' he said. 'You were my main rival when I was trying to seduce she-cats in the rue de Villejust.'

'Really?' I said quickly, before I could hide my surprise. It was too late then to keep up my superior act. 'It's just – well, I haven't been very lucky in love.'

'Who needs a lowly she-cat's love when you are an author's muse?' he said. 'That would be enough for me.'

Most – but not all – of the time it is, I thought. I followed him along the edges of the trenches, passing the quiet dugouts, moving towards the outer boundary of the line. It was a new-moon night, and very dark.

'Here, kitty, kitty,' one of the sentries said as we passed him, and he looked so relieved at discovering he was not entirely alone that we let ourselves be petted for a moment.

I could smell dog very strongly as we neared the next sentry point, and soon afterwards saw a massive, shaggy Berger de Brie just like the ones Colette had admired on a trip to Avignon with Missy. He was tied to a listening post on the firestep, so that he could just see over the edge of the trench. After growling faintly at us, the dog turned away and stared back into no man's land.

'His job is to sniff out Germans who might be raiding our line,' the tomcat whispered. 'They're starting to train these dogs in the Vosges. He's one of the first out here. Many of them can't master the trick of not barking to signal danger, but this one is the king of the low growl.'

The dog growled again and the soldier said quietly, 'Okay, boy, I've seen the cats. Ignore them.'

The dog growled more loudly, his nostrils dilated, his body tilted forward.

'Let's move away,' the tom said. 'I think he's trying to signal something else.'

We melted back into the trench.

Once again the dog growled, not moving his eyes from the direction of the German lines.

'I'm getting the commanding officer,' the soldier said to the dog, his breath visible in the overnight freeze. 'So this had better not be about those cats.' He left through the side warrens of the trench, and after a while returned with an officer who had clearly been sleeping in his uniform.

For a while the commanding officer stood and observed the dog's growling, his expression showing nothing but scepticism. 'You said there were cats,' the officer said.

'Yes, but he turned around to growl at them,' the sentry said. 'This is different. He's been focusing on that same point – to the left, ahead of us – for a while now.'

'I am not a believer in using dogs at the front,' the officer said. 'They're good for morale, but bad for strategy. Nothing but wartime pets.'

'Sir, I've never seen him like this before,' the sentry said. 'Could

we send up a flare? It might be somebody wounded and left for
dead, trying to make it back to the trenches. Or it could be a raid.'

The officer rubbed his eyes. 'Send one up,' he said. 'Then I'm
going back to bed.'

'Sir, we should wake our men, in case it's a raid,' the sentry said.

'Go on,' the officer said. 'You wake them. They hate me enough
already.'

The sentry went from soldier to soldier, rousing them with a
squeeze on the shoulder. They were alert instantly, accustomed to
being woken at night, and were soon lined up along the edge of the
trench with rifles ready. In a quick, skilled movement, the sentry
fired his flare pistol. The flare rose into the sky, a beautiful firework
illuminating the ghoulish line of our trenches beneath it, and not
far away, crouching in no man's land, five German soldiers instinc-
tively turned their young faces towards the light and froze. The dog's
whole body was trembling but he had not let the frightening pop of
the flare gun distract him. The soldiers in the trenches opened fire,
and did not stop until the flare's light began to dim as it floated back
to earth on its miniature parachute and the officer called for a halt.
Three of the German soldiers were dead. The other two had their
faces pushed into the mud, hands up in surrender.

The flare's last light showed the officer looking stunned. 'The
dog was right,' he said to the sentry. 'I will make sure he is mentioned in my dispatch to headquarters tomorrow.'

'After Paris was saved,' the sentry said, 'we heard that a pigeon
who'd carried a message crucial to our victory was awarded the
Légion d'honneur.' He was chatty now in his relief that the dog
hadn't been wrong. 'But the medal kept falling off from around his
neck, so they sewed bands with the colours of the medal's ribbon

around the bird's leg.'

The officer gave orders, and the prisoners were led away. The dog was still quivering.

The tom and I waited until the men had gone back to sleep, everyone except the sentry. We moved closer.

'You two almost got me in trouble,' he said, lighting a cigarette behind his helmet to keep its glowing end unseen across the lines.

The dog didn't bother growling this time. He looked exhausted.

'We hear you might be up for a medal,' the tom said to him from a cautious distance.

The dog put his head on his paws. 'I can finally run away and go home to my master and my sheep in Avignon without dishonour,' he said.

'But what about the parade in Paris?' the tomcat said. 'Haven't you heard? Any animal who's awarded a medal will be invited to be in it, once this war is over. It could be your grand moment!'

The dog closed his eyes. In the stillness the sentry's cigarette smoke moved upwards in an almost straight line.

'Let's go back to our trench,' I whispered to the tom.

'No, not yet. I have something to show you.'

'I thought the dog was it,' I said, following the tomcat out of the trench.

'He was the side-show.'

For a long time we prowled in silence, until we reached the final dugout at the edge of the line where a solitary soldier sat up awake, bent over a letter lit by a greenish-blue glow. I couldn't understand where the light was coming from until I saw the jar beside him, filled with glow-worms.

'They give these jars out sometimes, the night before a major offensive. They're supposed to be used for reading maps and battle-field plans. But he hides his jar during the day, and feeds them slugs to keep them alive,' the tom said. 'He stays up late, rereading letters from his sweetheart.'

'How do you know who they're from?' I asked.

'Sometimes he whispers them aloud,' he said.

I thought of how enchanted Colette would be by this little scene, and of the faraway look on her face while she writes by lamp-light, the only time I feel she is entirely lost to me. We used to come home from the Palmyre at the place Blanche after a supper of onion soup and small steaks, me beside her and Missy in the booth while they ate. At home, Colette would melt chocolate in a saucepan and dip a piece of rye bread in her cup. Then she'd call me by one of my pet names to sit on her lap in front of her writing desk: 'Come hither, Light of the Mountainside,' she would say, or, 'O little one, striped to the utmost, come warm my legs.'

I would go to her, and watch her closely as she slipped into her own mind to write. Sometimes she'd emerge again to read aloud to me a paragraph she had written. There is one from *La Vagabonde* that I resent, for it makes clear how far away from me she is in the deepest act of writing:

> To write is to sit and stare, hypnotised, at the reflection of the window in the silver inkstand, to feel the divine fever mounting to one's cheeks and forehead while the hand that writes grows blissfully numb upon the paper. It also means idle hours curled up in the hollow of the divan, and then an orgy of inspiration, from which one emerges stupefied and aching all over, but already recompensed, and laden with

treasures that one unloads slowly onto the virgin page in a little round pool of light under the lamp.

I used to wait there faithfully in the lamplight for her to return to me, but now – after this – would there be any nostalgic treasures left for her to unload onto a virgin page? Who would let her dwell on the comforts of autumn in Burgundy, or the idle imagined chatter of her pet dog and cat? There could be no room for frivolity in Paris, or anywhere, after this winter. And no room for me.

Sulphur and orange blossoms

In the night, my soldier lay beside his friend, hand in hand. I think they are in love but hide it from the other soldiers. I saw the very moment the air chose to glaze the world with frost, and it felt wrong to have witnessed this, as it had felt wrong to peek behind the curtain of the music-hall stage before Colette was fully in character, before her eyes had been ringed with blue grease. In the coldest part of the night, just before dawn, I came down into the trench and lay across my soldier's feet to keep him warm until the stand-to-arms.

For breakfast, the soldiers have been given boiled eggs. Poor Fufu – how her mouth must have been watering as the kitchen hands boiled egg after coveted egg! I thought of Colette's habit of eating hard-boiled eggs with fresh cherries. There was a whiff of sulphur in the trench as the soldiers rolled the eggs between palms to release their shells, and it took me in a sensory instant back to the Alpine trip she and I made between her performing tours to Brussels and Lyon. We stayed in the Hôtel des Bains and every morning when she led me for a walk in the park we could smell the sulphur rising from the hot springs where people came to take the waters.

Not Colette – she doesn't believe in bath cures, though she is fascinated by the self-involved neurotics who do. We would walk through the gardens, past the beds of geraniums and blue cinerarias, and behind the scent of orange blossom there was always lurking the uncomfortable smell of sulphur. We'd stop at the dairy stall in the park for fresh milk, which she would season for me with a pinch of sugar and a pinch of salt, and on our way back to the hotel the children and their nannies would call to me, 'Puss on the lead!' and want to give me things: balls with lead pellets inside them, or little pieces of stinky cheese. Such innocence! In them and in us.

I didn't mind being away from Paris, but I worried about Colette when she fell in with an odd couple staying at the hotel, as she tends to do, interested by their unhappiness. They in turn wanted to adopt her and me and were proud to be seen seated at her table in the dining room, the wrong sort of exhibitionist pride that comes from being seen in public with a person considered somewhat scandalous by society. I endured their company, and waited and longed for the morning she would finally grow bored of them and be ready to return to Paris. When she pulled out her suitcase I jumped into it as she was packing and joyfully kneaded each layer of her clothes with my claws. She knew exactly what I was doing, of course, for she spoke the words out loud. 'You are imploring me to blaze a trail just wide enough for my feet and for yours, a trail that will be obliterated behind us as we go,' she said. 'Isn't that right, Kiki, you whiskered tiger, fierce gatekeeper of my heart?'

Turtle derby

The tom woke me early this morning, quoting Colette. 'The cat is the animal to whom the Creator gave the biggest eye, the softest fur, the most supremely delicate nostrils, a mobile ear, an unrivalled paw and a curved claw borrowed from the rose-tree,' he said.

'I'm sleeping,' I said.

'Did you know,' he continued, 'that the Persians used to let cats loose on the battlefield when they were at war with the Egyptians? Since the Egyptians worshipped us, they'd always surrender rather than hurt the cats.'

I hissed at him and his anecdotal tinsel, wanting him to go away. No more silly little diversions, no more make-believe that I am still stretching out at my leisure on Colette's divan, no more creature comforts. We are at war now, all of us.

'I have news,' he said. 'I heard the soldiers talking about the sentry dog this morning. He made it safely hundreds of miles home. And when his master – who is apparently very loyal to the war effort – reported his return, the commander-in-chief not only awarded the dog a medal but gave him an honourable discharge from service!'

I felt terribly jealous of the dog all of a sudden, reunited with his master and his sheep.

The tom seemed to sense this. He changed tack. 'Do you like Colette's baby girl, Bel-Gazou?' he asked.

'What self-respecting cat likes a human baby!' I exclaimed.

'Is she a good mother?'

I hesitated. She is ambivalent about the role and has been from the start. She mused to me one summer evening, as we sat on the balcony and looked out across the pastel rooftops of Paris, 'How can I ever be a mother who happens to have written a book? I will always be, at heart, a writer who happens to have birthed a child.' I said nothing to the tom, not wanting to betray her secret: that she loves me more than she will ever love Bel-Gazou. I do not demand as much of her, and Colette, like all writers, is selfish with her time.

'I shouldn't have asked,' the tomcat said. 'I'll leave you alone.'

I thought for a long time about the dog's journey home, trying to imagine each stage of it, and wished I were a dog so that I could survive the same journey back to her in Paris, even if she no longer wants me, even if she has become serious in my absence, along with all those who have glimpsed the godforsaken future.

Eventually I went to find the tomcat in his trench. He made room for me next to him. We watched the soldiers bet on which mud turtle would win the slow-motion race they had been started on, from one side of the trench wall to the other. Three small turtles were plodding forward along the racing lanes the soldiers had created for them. A fourth was marching around and around in a determined circle, wearing a deep groove in the mud. And a fifth had somehow hoisted another turtle onto its back, and was winning the race.

Its preternatural strength reminded me of another trivial scene from years ago, before Colette's improving literary reputation allowed her to shift from music hall to theatre stage. She would take me with her to the Olympia or the Wagram Empire, or wherever she happened to be performing that season. I would lie across a spotlight in the wings until it became unbearably hot, watching each act from the darkness. One night I watched a sixteen-year-old girl, whose stage name was Jawbone, lift between her teeth a kitchen table with an enormously fat woman sitting on it.

The boredom on the faces of the soldiers betting on the trench turtle derby dissipated, to be replaced with alarm. They scattered, standing to attention. A shadow was thrown over me and the tom-cat. Somebody was standing in our sun at the entrance to the trench. I glanced up and saw Henri the sergeant, squinting as he tried to figure out exactly what he had caught the men doing.

'I heard about the dog,' he said to one of the soldiers. 'Was it the guard dog of this trench?'

'No, sir,' the soldier said. 'Several down along the line. But we gave it treats,' he added hopefully.

'Give a dog treats when men are starving?' he said. 'Shame on you.' His eyes had adjusted to the sunlight, and he now focused on us: two feline forms crouching in his shadow. 'Get these pests out of here,' he said. 'They'll spread disease.'

My brave, thin soldier stepped forward and tucked us under his arms. 'Sir, they catch the rats that bother us at night. And they lift our spirits.'

In the direct sunlight, I knew my fur would give me away. Henri had jealously listened to Colette go into raptures about my varied colours and stripes too many times for him not to recognise me. I looked into his eyes and he stared back at me, and I knew I'd been discovered.

'If I see those cats again, anywhere near these trenches,' he said, 'I will personally shoot them, then shoot any soldier found to be harbouring them.' He took another long look at me, letting his mal-ice bubble up into his gaze.

'That's her husband, isn't it?' the tomcat said when Henri had left.

My paws were sweating again. 'Yes,' I said.

'Come back only at night,' my soldier said. 'You are not safe here anymore.'

I purred and rubbed my cheek against his hand. Who was safe anywhere anymore?

'Let's go catch a carrier pigeon for lunch,' the tomcat said to me. 'It'll make you feel better.'

'I'm not the slightest bit hungry,' I said. I could feel my pulse beating in my throat, a sensation Colette once described when she was upset. 'I have to try to make it back to Paris.'

'I know,' he said. 'I've been waiting for you to realise this is what we need to do. We'll leave early tomorrow morning, at first light.'

A cheer rose from the other end of the trench. The smallest turtle had won the derby, carrying its friend on its back. The turtle that had chosen to go around in circles had dug such a deep trench for itself that it had successfully disappeared from view.

Going home

The tomcat insisted on night-hunting in no cat's land, as he calls it. He asked me to join him but I lied and said I wanted to preserve my strength for the start of our long journey to Paris. Really I just wanted to watch my soldier and his friend sleeping hand in hand on my final night in the trench. It's something I love to do with Colette: watch her sleep. If she wakes and catches me gazing at her, she offers me a treat, usually a moth caught between the window-pane and curtain.

I worry that my soldier will not survive this war. Colette would be better suited to life in the trenches than most of these skinny boys. She is robust and fit, her muscles kept flexible by regular sessions in her private gymnasium on the rue de Courcelles. At first it was to match the other performers in the music halls, who used their bodies in such bizarre ways that she felt she ought to strengthen her own. Then it became part of her weekly routine, especially once Missy was in her life: the two of them would put on shorts and headbands and do all kinds of stretches and exercises that made no physiological sense to me but seemed to make Colette happy and strong. On holiday at Missy's villa in the seaside town of Le Crotoy, the two of them would do their sessions on an outdoor gymnasium custom-built by Missy, shocking the passers-by.

Two carrier pigeons, both male, have crossed the night sky bearing a crucial message and are now flying in ovals as they try to orient themselves. They hate the dark. It is bewildering to see a pigeon silhouetted against the moon. A bat would better suit these sinister times. I think of the message I would send her if I could, imagine her unrolling it from the canister when the exhausted pigeon taps on her window: *In trying to stay close beside you, I have put great distance – an entire war – between us. But now I am coming home. Keep this bird for my dinner if you can.*

The tomcat should have returned by now. He promised he would be back before daylight. Colette always says there is a sad and suffocating difference between a room where a feline presence has a moment ago been reigning and the same room empty, and I feel that in this trench: a cold absence where the tomcat should be. It is clear to me what has happened and what will happen, but I cannot bring myself to move. Not quite yet, not with my soldier's feet beneath my belly. I will imagine movement instead, and perhaps these thoughts will take form and lead me towards the destiny that I sense is crouched waiting for me, not in the unreality of Paris but here in this trench.

I will wake the tomcat's adopted soldier from his slumber, and wait until he listens with enough concentration to hear the tom mewling from the mudlands in which he is trapped in wire. The soldier will crawl out to him without thinking of the dangers. The other soldiers will wait anxiously for his return, listening to the tomcat's cries, sick at the thought of the helpless creature in pain. As the sun begins to shade the sky a pale lemon, the soldier will return, shuffling on his stomach with the blinking tomcat tucked under one arm, both of them so covered in mud they could be two bits of the same mythical beast.

I will be waiting on the parapet, waiting for the tomcat, waiting for the sunlight, waiting for the moment a German sniper will mistake my glorious fur for a carelessly uncovered soldier's head, take aim, and fire. My own soldier and his friend will bring my body into the trench and grieve above me, and when my vision blurs they will look just like Colette and Missy dressed up as men. I will hear Colette saying that she and I must be curious until our final living moments, we must be determined to observe everything around us, that 'Look!' must be our final word and thought, and I will know that I have made it back to our little apartment, the one she and Toby-Chien and I used to share on the rue de Villejust, and I will know that I am almost home.

RED PETER'S LITTLE LADY

Soul of Chimpanzee

Died 1917, Germany

When I come home late at night from banquets, from scientific societies, or from social gatherings in someone's home, a small half-trained female chimpanzee is waiting for me, and I take my pleasure with her the way apes do. During the day I don't want to see her. For she has in her gaze the madness of a bewildered trained animal. I'm the only one who recognises that, and I cannot bear it.

Franz Kafka, A REPORT TO AN ACADEMY

Frau Evelyn Oberndorff
Tierparkallee 55
Hamburg

June 13th, 1915

My dear Evelyn

   I know you said not to write to you, not ever again. But time has passed, and a war has been started, and Herr Hagenbeck told me in no uncertain terms that I should write to Hazel care of you, that she has come a long way since your husband began working with her, and it would be appropriate now for me to be in closer touch with her. 'She is being prepared to become your wife, in due course,' Herr Hagenbeck said to me, in that manner he has of making one feel unaccountably guilty. He also gave me the distressing news that Herr Oberndorff has gone to the front. I am truly sorry to hear it. I am even more sorry that in his absence, Hazel's training has fallen to you. It cannot be easy. And here I am making it worse, asking you to read this letter below aloud to her.

Yours
Red Peter

Dear Hazel

I chose this name for you at our first encounter at the zoological garden, many years ago, for the colour of your eyes in your wide, empty face. You may not remember me; my name, as you will come to know, is Red Peter – Red for my fur, Peter for my first trainer back in Prague.

I shall send this letter directly to your new trainer, Frau Oberndorff, who has stepped in while her husband is away. She will be reading my letters aloud to you for now, though it sounds as if your progress with reading and writing is beyond expectations. I am pleased to hear from our benefactor, Herr Hagenbeck, that your comprehension and speaking skills are already quite remarkable.

What to say, what else to tell you? My pipe is filled, a book of poetry lies at the foot of my armchair. I am looking out of my hotel window at the streets of Hamburg, watching dusk's possibilities evaporate. My thoughts have snagged on old Peter, my namesake, the man who taught me to read. He is probably no longer alive. He was white-haired and kind, and took me along to see Halley's Comet cross the sky, trapped in its oblong orbit, in 1910. We watched from the dome of the observatory, built above a bastion of Prague's medieval Hunger Wall, with a small group of young literary dandies to whom I owe my sense of style.

One was called Blei, another Kafka. The former took no notice of me. But Kafka, very thin, looked me directly in the eye. It was no moment of communion. He was envious of me, I think, of my small existence, and my ability to become almost invisible to humans at certain times. He lay down near me on the stone floor to watch the comet pass, which made me uncomfortable.

I remember what he said to his companions that night as they left to walk home. 'Had I not been lying on the ground among the animals, I would have been unable to see the sky and the stars. Perhaps I wouldn't have survived the terror of standing upright.'

The terror of standing upright, my dear, is something you will soon have to survive yourself. Do believe me that it is worth it. The view is much better from up here.

Sincerely
Red Peter

Dear Red Peter

I enclose Hazel's reply to your recent letter. I have tried to use her own dictated words as much as possible. She is coming along quickly now, as Herr Hagenbeck has informed you, and I am particularly pleased with her word play. Forgive her occasional coarseness, if you can. She has made a big leap recently, allowing me to dress her in an evening dress and small shoes without too much protest. It was the bodice that gave her the most trouble. The frustration with her body that she expresses should be seen as a positive step, I believe, as it can only motivate her to give up her chimpanzee habits and fully embrace human ways – as you have, to such astounding effect.

My husband is indeed at the front. It was his choice to go, I should tell you, though men may not have the luxury of choice for much longer, not even family men. The children miss him dreadfully.

Evelyn Oberndorff

Dear Red Peter

What use is this body to anyone? Why can my nostrils not be small as pips? Why does hair grow on my back? Frau Oberndorff gives me exercises to do by the window in the laboratory. Calisthenics, she calls them, for a new body. I do what she says, for the ginger biscuits. They make my shit dark and hard.

I saw women throwing boiled sweets and chocolate and fruit to the soldiers in the streets. My first taste of chocolate. I asked Frau

Oberndorff why everybody is happy. The people are glad for a break in their routines, they are bored of life, she said. They think it is exhilarating to be at war. Exhilarating. A new word for me. New body, new word, new war. I ate too much chocolate and afterwards felt sick.

Regards
Hazel

Dear Evelyn

       I thank you for your reply, and for Hazel's dictated note. I see I was asking too much in addressing you with familiarity, but when I sit down to write to you it is impossible to hold back. These years banished from you have been terrible. To know that you are holding in your hands this piece of paper, that you are reading these words . . . I cannot pretend to be formal. Forgive me, Evelyn, for everything. Please give my love to the children. I miss them. I miss you.

Yours
Red Peter

Dear Hazel

       How glad I am to hear that you have embraced our new, healthful German body culture. Let me tell you of my own regime, in case it may help you build your body into what you would like it to be.

       Do not eat too much chocolate, I warn you. It can only lead to unhappiness. Many years ago, I decided to follow a strict dietary regimen to maximise my health, after years of suffering from ailments (back pain, migraines, sleeplessness). A stay at the sanatorium in the Harz Mountains introduced me to Mueller's body-building program, which Frau Oberndorff has wisely started you on, and to this day I do my exercises (as you do) before an open window. Lately, I have begun to feel the benefits of exercising nude outdoors, but this I do not yet counsel for yourself. One should only venture into nudism when one has learned to wear clothes.

I follow the Fletcher program of chewing every bite of food more than ten times. I am thin now, thinner than most humans I know, and it pleases me to be this way, without the least bit of fat on my body. Try, if you can, to eat *mindfully*. It will help you to overcome your instincts to fill your stomach to bursting with whatever is at hand. Eat slowly, never crack bones with your teeth if you must eat meat, do not sip vinegar noisily.

I refuse tea, coffee and alcohol. Contrary to what you might think, this discipline I impose on myself does not make me the slightest bit envious of other people's pleasure in indulgences. The opposite, in fact. If I am sitting at a table with ten friends all drinking black coffee while I drink none, the sight of it gives me a feeling of happiness. Meat can be steaming around me, mugs of beer drained in huge draughts, those juicy sausages can be cut up all over the place – all this and worse gives me no sensation of distaste whatever; on the contrary, it does me a great deal of good. There is no question of my taking a malicious pleasure in it.

Think of it like this. Have you been told the story of how Herr Hagenbeck decided to create a zoo without bars, so that visitors could gaze across the ditch separating them from the animals in their open-air panoramas? No bars to get in the way of a good wondrous stare, no cages to keep the animals from full expression of their wild selves.

What you need to do now is put those bars back in place, so to speak, in your heart and stomach and mind. Hem yourself in again, deny yourself whatever you desire, until the pleasure comes from the denial itself, not the consummation of the desire. Only then will you be truly free, and closer to human. They – the humans, that is – seem to think that what sets them apart from other animals is their ability to love, grieve, feel guilt, think abstractly, et cetera. They are misguided. What sets them apart is their talent for masochism. Therein lies their power. To take pleasure in pain, to derive strength from deprivation, is to be human.

Sincerely
R.P.

Dear Red Peter

I hope this short dictated reply from Hazel finds you well. I understand from Herr Hagenbeck that you do not want to visit the zoo and meet with Hazel again until she is ready to be a companion worthy of you. Forgive my impertinence, but could you ask your gentlemen friends to refrain from visiting too? They come here – the ones who have not gone to war, for one reason or another – and knock on the laboratory door, making sly insinuations about Hazel being expertly prepared for your enjoyment, and they demand to see her. I remind them that she is to be your life's companion, and ask them to show respect. But I would rather they didn't visit and left us in peace until you are ready to debut her yourself.

The children know that you are writing to Hazel. They asked why you aren't writing to them, and I didn't know what to say. I am having a hard enough time explaining where their father is.

You are wrong about humans and masochism, by the way (do I imagine that your letters to Hazel are full of barbs for me?). Most of us derive no pleasure from pain; most of us persist in the belief that romantic love is the shimmering jewel in the crown of human evolution. Some among us suffer to think of your open window, the cool evening air floating through it, the warmth of your body beneath the covers.

Evelyn

Dear Red Peter

The zoo, so noisy, my own thoughts held out. The birds in their enclosure squawk day and night. I am itchy. Itchy, itchy, itchy. Frau Oberndorff won't let me scratch. She bathes me, combs my hair to make it lie down, cuts my toenails, cleans my tear ducts. She says my breath is a problem. It stinks. I like the stink. I breathe out and sniff it in. I cling to the lamp that hangs from the ceiling and swing on it, back and forth, back and forth. I scratch my bum, sniff my fingers.

How did you become what you are? Why do you want me?

Regards
Hazel

My dearest Evelyn

            Your letter lit a fire in my heart, a hopeful bright burn . . .

I am sorry that my acquaintances (I would not call them friends) have been bothering you at the zoo.

Do you still not believe me, darling? That Hazel was all Hagenbeck's idea, that I was forced to go along with his plan as I have been forced to do everything he wanted of me for his cursed zoo? That if I had a choice, if *you* had a choice – you are somebody else's wife, let us not forget – I would choose you, you and only you? I fell in love with you the first moment I saw you, before I was fully human, and from across that gulf of understanding and experience, somehow, miraculously, you felt something for me in return. You alone inspired me to become human, not your husband's relentless mazes and sorting tasks and word repetitions, not his tantrums when I didn't do what he wanted, not the whipping, not the sweet fruit he dangled just out of my reach. I wanted to be human so that I might reach out across that chasm and touch you, be touched by you. You made me a better human, and I would like to think – dare I say it? – that I made you a better ape.

Yours always
R.P.

Dear Hazel

In your last letter you asked for my own tale of transformation, and so I offer it. Do not be discouraged. It is a long process, beset with difficulty, to become human.

I have only dim memories of our natal home. Fragments. Perhaps you remember more. A thicket of wild blossoms that sprouted in the forest after the heaviest of night thunderstorms. The sensation of being gripped by a boa constrictor, the pressure comforting; almost giving in to death's lullaby before I was rescued – by my mother? my sister? – from the tightening coil. I have a scar along my hipbone from the hunter's dart, but I don't remember being shot. On the ship, they hung bananas from the top of my cage as a game but I refused to eat them. Then Prague, being fitted for a red velvet waistcoat and matching hat for my first appearance at the theatre. Peter's gentleness. The curtain opening on us sitting side by side on stage, reading beneath a spotlight, and suddenly the intimate moment being exposed for what it was: a performance for a raucous crowd.

Herr Hagenbeck bought me from Peter on one of his visits to Prague. He could see what I might be capable of, in a way that Peter could not. Hagenbeck enlisted Oberndorff, the ethologist, to train me here in Hamburg. His colleagues ridiculed him, but he ignored them, for they had also laughed at his attempts to cross a leopard with a Bengal tiger at the turn of the century, until he sold the successful hybrid for an unfathomable sum to a Portuguese collector.

I spent several years in the same laboratory at the zoological garden where you are now. Herr Oberndorff was very strict in his training regimes, brutal even, as you would already know. But Frau

Oberndorff and the children made up for this in every possible way. I grew to love them deeply.

My human skills progressed so quickly that even Herr Oberndorff was shocked one day to see me strolling through the grounds beside Herr Hagenbeck, discussing politics and philosophy. Soon after that, I was moved into the city's best lodgings, and began to attract record numbers of visitors to the zoo with my speaking engagements and public lectures.

Which brings me to your second question: why do I want *you*? For some time I have needed a companion to accompany me in a dignified manner to gatherings and embassy functions, to Academy dinners, to special occasions frequently held in my honour around Hamburg. You were selected from the enclosure of chimpanzees at the zoo and did exceptionally well on the initial aptitude tests. Herr Hagenbeck decided that you too should be trained to be human, and that you would one day become my wife.

Then there is the matter of the other comfort you will bring, in becoming my companion. It did not seem fitting to Herr Hagenbeck for me to take a human wife for this purpose, nor could I bring myself to overcome my horror of the primitive chimpanzees at the zoo. My one fear – surely nothing worse can either be said or listened to – is that I shall never be able to possess you . . . I would sit beside you and feel the breath and life of your body at my side, yet in reality be further from you than now, here in my room. Let us not dwell on this, however. These thoughts still make me a little queasy (forgive me).

Sincerely
R.P.

Dear Red Peter

You will be glad to hear that Hazel has been accompanying me on excursions out of the laboratory, into the city itself. She no longer pulls off her clothes at every opportunity and she keeps her hat on for an extended period. She is comfortably walking upright, and people around me smile at her as if she were one of my children in her bonnet and dainty shoes. Her speaking and comprehension skills are rapidly becoming sophisticated. Herr Hagenbeck feels that she will be ready for you far sooner than expected. My husband would be delighted at her progress, the fruits of his labour. I have not had a return letter from him at the front for many months now.

Do you remember when my eldest child first began to talk in full sentences, how he would verbalise his thoughts without realising it? I used to eavesdrop on these 'conversations', glad to have a direct line into my son's mind after years of guessing in a parent's hopeful way at his needs and heart's desires. You were here then, you liked to eavesdrop with me. You had only just started talking in full sentences yourself.

Hazel is in the middle of a similar phase, I think. Yesterday I eavesdropped on her in the laboratory and heard her wondering aloud to herself, 'Am I more similar to a hedgehog or to a fox?' I had to have a little laugh before going in to her. It helped me forget our collective troubles, for an hour at least.

Did you send that old Chinese man to the zoo last week? I suspect you did. He gave me a copy of Buber's recent book of Chinese tales. And a pet cricket, a creature of whimsy. I gave the cricket to

Hazel. She likes looking after small creatures. She is a gentle soul.

And yes, if you are wondering – I do remember that night, reading Buber together, and everything else.

Yours
Evelyn

Dear Red Peter

Frau Oberndorff gave me a pet cricket. The cricket lives in a walnut shell. If you hold him up and look at him directly, he looks fierce. The man who brought the cricket to the zoo said he would win battles against other crickets if we first chop up a fly and feed it to him to make him violent.

I went with Frau Oberndorff and the children to stand in the ration lines. One line for each item, a long wait in a line for the weekly allowance of a single egg. Another line, another long wait for the war bread made of fodder turnips. It gives the children sore stomachs.

My ears are pierced with metal studs to make me beautiful. I can pull on stockings without laddering them. But there are no longer any stockings to be had.

Regards
Hazel

My dearest Evelyn

I am glad the book of Chinese tales and the cricket were able to distract you for a moment from the misery of recent events. Does Hazel understand what is happening, why food has suddenly become so scarce? I am sure you have explained to her already, but I will also mention it in my letter, in case that helps.

I am worried about you and the children. Do you have enough to eat? Is Herr Hagenbeck helping you to source milk and meat on the black market? I wish I could send you supplies, but to be frank, I am not having much luck finding extra myself. The waiters in the hotel dining room have started giving me looks when I come down from my rooms to eat the one meagre daily meal they still provide. Perhaps I am imagining it. Luckily, as you know, I don't eat much. I am grateful to have trained myself into this frugality years ago. It would be beastly to be beholden to something as basic as food at such a time.

Yours
Red Peter

Dear Hazel

In the interests of your education you should try to grasp what is happening to Germany. The pernicious effects of the British naval blockade, which has cut off the flow of foodstuffs to Germany from the North Sea, are now being felt. For too long we have been importing over a third of our food this way, and most of our fertiliser too, and now we are in trouble. The worldwide drought and crop failure has made it much worse. It goes far beyond a line of women waiting for eggs in the cold. There are strikes and food riots breaking out in our major cities. Food is being used as a weapon against us. England wants to squeeze the German lemon until the pips squeak. And we, my dear, are the pips.

Sincerely
R.P.

Dear Red Peter

I do not want to worry you – we are fine, mostly. But food is scarce, as you say, and we are struggling to find enough to feed the animals at the zoo. The children and I are surviving on dark bread, a few slices of sausage with no fat, and three pounds of turnips a week. My daughter stole a pound of butter from another child on the street and my younger son looted a stringy piece of boiled beef and we celebrated this with more enthusiasm than if Germany had won the war. Of course we share any food we have with Hazel.

I'm afraid Herr Hagenbeck has not helped us to buy any food on the black market. He has not been to the zoo in a while now. I do not want to disrespect him, and perhaps he is trying as we speak to source extra supplies – but if you see him out in the city at one of the Academy functions, will you remind him of us, and of the animals?

Hazel's latest letter, as you will see, is a little uncouth. But again, in the interests of allowing her free rein to explore and experiment with language, I have noted down, word for word, what she dictated to me. She was quite taken with *The Entropy of Reason* – I have been reading to her from the copy you gave me years ago. I hope her letter does not embarrass you. It shouldn't. She is quite right about what she can give you. Things that I could not.

Yours
Evelyn

Dear Red Peter

How will we play bedroom games when I am your wife? Frau Oberndorff is reading Dr Mitzkin's book to me, *The Entropy of Reason*. He warns that humans will be reduced to word machines. They will eat words, drink words, bathe in words, imprison themselves with words, kill themselves with words. Copulate with words.

Will you toss words at me when I swing from the curtains towards you and display my arsehole? Will I throw words at you when you thump your chest and sink your fangs into my rump? I cannot give you much other than a warm body flexible in the ways you would like it, a certain length of arm, bow legs, a barrel torso. Would you like me to be more human, or less human, or more or less human?

Regards
Hazel

Dearest Evelyn

You must let me visit you. Please, darling, don't be stubborn about this. I need to know that you and the children are all right. Do not worry about Herr Hagenbeck finding out – he has gone to Africa to sit out the war, according to rumours among my colleagues at the Academy. I couldn't believe at first that he would abandon the zoo after his considerable financial investment in it (and in me), but I suppose it makes sense. He is a man who puts his own needs first and this has always stood him in very good stead. There will be other exotic animals, other zoos, other apes to train.

I feel sorry for Hazel, truly I do, but now that Hagenbeck is gone, I won't be forced into it anymore. Not just writing to her, but everything, the whole terrible partnership he dreamed up for me. He is gone, Evelyn, he is gone. We are free – almost – to do as we please.

I want to see you. Please. Take me back.

Yours
Red Peter

Dear Red Peter

Thank you for sending us a bushel of potatoes, which we devoured. The children would have eaten them raw if I had not stopped them descending on the sack just in time.

You were right about Herr Hagenbeck. He has indeed abandoned the zoo and gone to Africa. A letter arrived from him today, mailed in Hamburg before he left. After all these years, after all that we have done for him, this is what he had to say:

> I must remind you that the incidence of actual starvation in Hamburg is extremely low. The only known cases so far, even through this harsh winter, have been among the inmates of jails, asylums, and other institutions where each adult has access only to war rations, unsupplemented by black market supplies.
>
> My good friend Dr Neumann, Professor of Hygiene at the University of Bonn, has just sent me the results of his most interesting experiment. He limited himself for a month to the food ration for an average person. The outcome is that he lost a third of his weight and was so hungry he found it difficult to concentrate on his work.
>
> But who among us – other than prisoners and madmen – cannot find what he or she needs to survive beyond the official rations? I do believe it is a way of separating the wheat from the chaff, so to speak.
>
> This communal hunger is bringing out our ingenuity as a nation. Take, for example, our efforts to engineer alternative edible fats now that vegetable fats are being reserved for the manufacture of glycerine for propellants and explosives. Industry has stepped in to provide all kinds of solutions: bones are steamed, grease is squeezed from old rags or household slops, oil is wrung from graphite and from seeds and fruit stones. Flavourful berries and leaves are steeped

in hot water for tea. We have even invented a surrogate for beer using chemicals rather than malt. Trust in our German nation. We shall prevail.

He shall prevail, no doubt, sitting in the lush jungle in Africa while we starve in Hamburg!

Hazel has insisted on writing to you this week, though you did not write to her. Her thoughts have taken a turn for the poetic, one could say. What follows is closer to impressions one might jot down in a diary. I have persisted in recording them for you, however, as I believe she is going through another important linguistic developmental phase.

You cannot visit us, not now. My husband wrote to say he will soon be returning on leave.

Evelyn

The trip into the city. Frau Oberndorff's face. She runs her fingers through her hair, wipes her nose, yawns with hunger. Her hair has gone dull, no colour in her lips, bloodless.

She took me and the children to the soup kitchen at the Children's Home. The youngest child may have turnip disease. The children were given a meal of thin soup made from mangold-wurzel and cabbage, and stock from stewed horse bones. It smelled disgusting and they tell me it tasted worse.

A doctor working at the Home pointed out to Frau Oberndorff a boy orphan with a swollen stomach. He had a broken jaw and was missing most of his teeth due to rickets. 'You see this child here, it was given an incredible amount of bread and yet it did not get any stronger,' the doctor said. 'I found out that it hid all the bread it received underneath its straw mattress. The fear of hunger was so deeply rooted in the child that it collected the stores instead of eating the food. A misguided animal instinct made the dread of hunger worse than the actual pangs.'

The bedbug. Hard decision to squash and eat it, and not give it to my cricket for his supper. But I was very hungry.

My darling Evelyn

Thank you, thank you, a thousand times, for yesterday. I suspect when you saw me standing at the door your first instinct was to slam it shut, and if it hadn't been for the children's joy at seeing me, I would not have been invited inside. I was shocked to see you looking so thin, my dear. I scoured the city for black market supplies this morning, with no success – some of the people waiting in a ration queue threw stones at me when they saw me lurking nearby. Nobody wants to see an ape eat when there are humans going hungry.

I want to say that you have done well with Hazel. She is sweet, and very clever. She should not fear her fate now that Herr Hagenbeck is no longer here to force our union. I agree with you that her intensive training should be stopped for now – there are more important things for all of us to worry about – and when your husband returns he can decide how to proceed. Is it strange that I think of her as one of your children? Perhaps we could care for her as such in the future.

Do not worry, darling, I will stay away now that you are expecting your husband to return any day. The single touch of your smooth hands as you said goodbye will sustain me.

R.P.

Dear R.P.

I have troubling news of Hazel. A few days ago she found your notes to me, enclosed in the same envelopes containing the letters for her. She can read quite well now, though how much she understood of their full meaning I am not certain. Since then, she has stopped eating. She refuses all food I offer her, and has retreated to her old cage at the back of the laboratory, where she used to live before she learned her manners. I am hoping this is a temporary side effect of extreme hunger – eating simply makes one hungry again; not eating at least does not give the stomach false hope. However, I thought it best to let you know.

As I asked you in person, please do not write until you hear from me again, just in case.

Yours
Evelyn
PS: Hazel refused to dictate a letter to you. I'm sorry.

Dear Red Peter

Perhaps you have already heard. My husband is dead. He did not make it home from the front. It is no use pretending; you know how I felt about him. I will not miss his cold rage. But I grieve for my younger guileless self, the girl I was when I agreed to marry him. And for the children. They don't understand, not really. We are all distracted by our hunger. Strong emotion uses up a lot of energy, and we don't have much of it anymore.

I haven't told Hazel. She was always partial to him, despite his cruel training methods. We are out of coal for heating, and my little household's supplies of both petroleum and methyl alcohol are almost used up. The colder and darker it becomes in the lab, the stronger Hazel's will seems to be to remain within her cage. The children and I try to keep her company in there as often as we can, when we are not standing in the ration lines.

I have cut up the few clothes my husband left behind – they had been hanging uselessly in the cupboard since he left – and made small towels for the children out of them. We were down to a single bath towel for the whole family to use. I have impetigo rash from wearing the same unwashed wool suit for weeks, but there is no soap to be had.

Hazel dictated the note below to you. She is still not herself; she is not thinking clearly. Nothing I can do or say will induce her to eat.

Give me some time, darling, to pull myself together before you visit.

Yours
Evelyn

Did you get yourself a bit of pork in the recent Pig Murders, Red Peter? A fair share of the fatty spoils? I hear the pigs were so skinny there was almost nothing on them. Nine million hogs ordered slaughtered by the government to give everybody a break from months of meatlessness.

Of course, how could I forget? You don't eat meat.

Dearest Evelyn

I am sorry I disregarded your plea and came to see you the very day I received the letter about your husband. But I am not sorry for taking you in my arms and kissing you, tasting your tears, feeling your ribs pressed against mine. I am hungry, darling, starving, but only for you.

In my delirious joy at holding you again I forgot to apologise for my appearance. Since the American cotton shortage, and the decree that men can no longer keep more than two suits of clothing, the police decided to enter my rooms at the hotel and requisitioned my suits from the wardrobe, and I have had some trouble finding suitable attire since. I don't think I was specifically targeted, not this time at least. At the Academy I have heard stories about how dire this shortage is. A colleague told me of a soldier at the front who was issued a shirt made from a woman's winter blouse, gathered with a ribbon around his neck. He refused it, and said he would rather die of cold in a shirt made of paper.

For the first time in many years, I find myself grateful to have fur. It seems this war is slowly stripping me of the trappings of being human, thread by thread. But that is fine, as long as I am never again stripped of you.

Yours always
Red Peter

Dearest R.P.

The boots you found for my little girl to keep her feet warm while she is unwell fit her perfectly. The varnish on the paper uppers has cracked a little, but nothing I can't fix.

Hazel's fasting has continued. She asked me to put a sign outside her cage, and dictated what I should write on it: THE HUNGER ART-IST. She must have picked that up from the man Herr Hagenbeck hired to fast at the zoo a few years ago, as a summer diversion. Now she wants me to charge spectators a small fee to stand outside her cage and watch her starve, but we do not have many paying visitors to the zoo these days. People get angry when they see animals being fed, even if it is with turnip peels – but you know this already. She has dictated another note for you. I fear she is losing her mind, but whether it is from hunger or as a delayed consequence of her training, I cannot tell.

I can hardly wait to see you again tomorrow.

Yours
Evelyn

There was once a Hunger Artist who kept the good people of Stellingen and Hamburg entertained by fasting for forty days and forty nights.

Do you remember him? Perhaps you visited the zoo on one of your speaking rounds and stopped outside the enclosure where he sat cross-legged in little more than a loincloth? Naughty boys liked to tempt the Artist to eat by throwing peanuts into his enclosure, but the nuts remained untouched in their woody shells. Visitors believed he was creating a masterpiece with his own body.

But then the people lost interest. Nobody bought season tickets anymore, nobody came in the evenings to watch him starve by torchlight. Even the man he had employed as his professional watcher, to guarantee to spectators that he was not secretly gorging himself overnight, quit his job. Is there anything more ridiculous than an Artist who suffers without an audience? Nobody was there on the forty-first day, when the Hunger Artist crawled out of his cage and sat in the sun to eat an apple.

The creatures around me are no longer being fed. They would do anything – anything – for food; in fact they debase themselves daily begging for it. Does it matter now? That some of us will die of disease, some of malnutrition, some of exposure? We will all die hungry, but only I will have *chosen* to starve. The humans are no better. Their bonds are too fragile, held together by not much more than shared food on a table. Is that all that lies between the behaviour of apes and humans? A regular supply of hot meals?

My thoughts have become an endless source of fascination.

I can watch them traipse across my own mind in a parade of startling brilliance. How everything can be ventured; how a fire is ready for all ideas, however strange, in which they burn up and are resurrected! In the corner of my cage, I breathe in the sweet rot of leaves. My cricket chirps at the moon from the warmth of his walnut. The light turns blue before the window. I hope they heat me up and eat me.

My dearest Evelyn

Perhaps you are right that this is the safest place for me to wait out the war, now that the authorities have chased me out of my hotel rooms. But still it feels as if I have regressed – sitting here in this empty cage in the laboratory, unclothed, without my pipe to calm me with a twist of white smoke. I can sense Hazel's apish presence here. Her smell is all over the leaves even if she herself is gone. I'm sorry, my dear, but I have to say, she stank to high heaven! Or perhaps, horror, horror, horror, I am simply smelling myself. I don't know anymore. I am scribbling on this scrap of paper, waiting for your night visit impatiently, as I used to. But this letter writing is no use, it is an intercourse between ghosts – the ghost of the receiver and one's own ghost, which emerges between the lines of the letter being written . . . kisses on paper never reach their destination, they are drunk up en route by these ghouls. I cannot stop thinking of how you fed me a spoonful of pumpkin marmalade this morning from the can that was sold to each household at Christmas, meant to last your family an entire year. You held it out, the spoon, through the bars of the cage, and waited for me to lick the marmalade off. I did. You said you wanted to fatten me up. And immediately I knew I had made a terrible mistake getting back into this cage. Don't let us miss our chance, darling! Unlock this cage, let me out, let me into your bed!

HUNDSTAGE

Soul of Dog

Died 1941, Poland

*Those who are humane toward animals are not necessarily
kind to human beings.*

Boria Sax, ANIMALS IN THE THIRD REICH

*But whom, I asked, do I really want
singly and in fistfuls
to destroy until nothing is left?*

*First of all yourself, said the She-rat.
In the beginning self-destruction
was practised only in private.*

Günter Grass, THE RAT

How do I begin to describe my beloved Master and my life with
him before I was exiled to the woods?

On the day I was presented to him, he was in his magnificent
office overlooking the larch trees that were beginning to turn, weeping over a dead canary. I watched as he placed the bird's body in a tin
and gave it to a servant to bury in a special lot within the grounds.

His sorrow eased as we began to play. He did not tire as humans
normally do after a while, and took pleasure in the cinnamon smell
of my puppy breath. It struck me for the first time that it was a privilege to be a companion species to humans, a term the scientists at
the Society had often used.

My possessiveness gratified him. In each meeting my Master attended, I sat at his feet under the table, waiting for the agreeable weight of his hand on my head.

One late autumn morning after he had walked me in the forest, I lay beside him in front of the fire to listen to a radio address by a man whom my Master seemed to respect. This man announced that animals were no longer to be experimented on without limits, or killed without concern for our suffering. He said something very beautiful: 'To the German, animals are not merely creatures in the organic sense, but creatures who lead their own lives and who are endowed with perceptive facilities, who feel pain and experience joy and prove to be faithful and attached.'

I heard a sound from my Master. He was crying, moved by these words. I licked away his tears, and that made them fall more swiftly.

My sister Blondi and I were raised on stories about our grand-father, one of the first of our kind. Our breed was the invention of the scientist von Stephanitz, who believed he was recreating a modern version of the Germanic wolf-dogs that once roamed these conifer forests. Grandfather had taken this responsibility seriously, though he confided to us before he died that he had not known as a young dog how he was meant to behave, what exactly the humans expected of him.

As he moved beyond the generic playfulness of his puppy days, he had sensed von Stephanitz's impatience for him to express more particularly his curated genes. Grandfather decided to try being alert and aloof, and all the humans who came to observe him were impressed. Over time, he experimented with other qualities and fine-tuned them. He didn't lunge at his food, for this seemed to disappoint von Stephanitz by suggesting greed, and he never bonded too quickly with any new human, for von Stephanitz interpreted this as disloyalty. Aggression in the right circumstances was admired, and desire for females was tolerated as long as he only coupled with purebreds. One lonely night, my grandfather howled at the full moon, and von Stephanitz took this as proof of the wolf blood in our breed's veins.

Grandfather's lowest moment – an incident that was not recorded in any research notebooks – was being caught behind a bitch of unknown breeding kept in the same facility for canine medication experimentation, whose hair and teeth had fallen out. He felt the burden then of being the ur-type, and swore off females until von Stephanitz guided my beautiful grandmother into his pen.

A few months after our birth, Blondi and I were taken away from the rest of our litter at the Society for Animal Psychology, and transported to a lodge in the woods far outside the city. We had heard of other young dogs from the Society being taken out into these woods, where they were kept on a leash to avoid breaking one of the humans' new laws on animal protection, banning the use of dogs in the fox chase. The scientists at the Society were very proud of this law, and of the many others we had heard them discuss at their meetings. Yet it was not until Blondi and I met our new Masters that we began to understand the significance of these laws, and the fullness of our Masters' compassion for animals. At the lodge, she was presented to the human leader of our country, and I was given to one of his close associates.

My Master was having a massage – his masseur came once a week to knead the tension out of his body – while I lay beneath the chaise longue, breathing in the scent of clove oil. I was starving. My Master had recently begun to follow a vegetarian diet and decided that I should give up all meat too, in keeping with his beliefs, for it offended his sensibilities to see me gobble down a bloody steak while he ate lettuce and herbs for lunch. Not only that, he was concerned about my karma. He had promised me that if I did as he said, ate no meat, resisted my urge to hunt foxes, and tried to meditate once a day, I might be reincarnated as a human being in my next life. A human being! The thought was intoxicating.

'Herr Kersten,' my Master was saying to his masseur, who was an avid hunter, 'how can you possibly shoot from an ambush at the poor animals which are grazing so innocently, defenselessly and unawares at the edge of the woods? If you take the right view of your action, it is murder pure and simple. Nature is very beautiful, and after all, every animal has a right to live.'

Herr Kersten said nothing, only grunted a little as he worked on my Master's tight shoulders.

'It is this point of view which I admire so much in our ancestors,' my Master continued. 'Respect for animals is something you find in all Indo-Germanic people. It interested me terribly to hear the other day that Buddhist monks still wear little bells when they walk through the forest, so that the creatures on whom they might step have a chance to get out of the way. But here everyone steps on worms and snails without giving it a second thought.'

I was listening closely, as usual, for my Master liked to tell Herr Kersten about his philosophical beliefs. Something about being half naked in a heated room filled with the scent of essential oils made him talkative, and Herr Kersten was a good listener – he did not interrupt, and he never asked my Master to repeat himself, even if his words were sometimes a little blurry because his face was pressed into the cushions.

'You may not know this, Herr Kersten,' my Master said, 'but I used to be a chicken farmer in my previous life. That's right. I used to chop off chicken heads as easily as one, two, three. Then somebody gave me Hermann Hesse's book *Siddhartha*. Have you read it?'

Herr Kersten dug his knuckles into the knots in my Master's neck, making the small bones click. 'No, Herr Himmler, I have not.'

'It is remarkable. It's set in ancient India and based on the life of the Buddha. After I finished it, I wanted to know more about Hinduism, and Professor Wüst, who is an expert in this field and my spiritual guide, suggested I read the Bhagavad Gita, one of the Hindu scriptures. It tells of the adventures of the world's greatest warrior, Arjuna, and the guidance his god Krishna gives him along the way. It helped me realise that the rotten luck I'd been having in my life was because of all the bad karma I attracted from killing chickens. I read passages from it each night before bed.'

I thought of the few chickens I had managed to kill and eat in my life before becoming a vegetarian, and felt sick. And hungry. I thought of how good their blood tasted, of how prettily their feathers floated through the air.

The other appointment my Master kept without fail, every other week, was his meditation sessions with Professor Wüst, held in the sacred crypt beneath the north tower of the castle at Wewelsburg. I loved going there because, on rare occasions, I would see Blondi accompanying her Master to the castle and we would be allowed to play together in the grounds, or in the circular entrance hall, where we liked to try to dig out the Black Sun embedded in the marble floor. Sometimes we were allowed to visit others of our kind in the settlement nearby – relatives and friends who had also been bred and trained at the Society, who were working as guard dogs, making sure that the slaves who were carrying out my Master's grand reno-vations of the castle did their work properly. Our favourite place of all was the castle crypt itself, huge and dark, with a single flame that never stopped burning. If we barked down there, the sound was tre-mendous; dozens of dogs barked back at us out of nowhere.

If Blondi wasn't at the castle, I would stand watch beside my Master and Professor Wüst while they sat cross-legged on the crypt's stone floor to meditate in silence. Afterwards they would talk through aspects of their beliefs so that my Master could in turn provide strong spiritual guidance to his underlings.

On my final visit to Wewelsburg – it was the last time I was to accompany my Master to the castle before my betrayal, before my banishment – he and Professor Wüst, after meditating for some time, began to discuss how to inspire their followers to be coura-geous in battling our enemies, for a war had been declared, and Germany was destined to win it.

'I have been giving this some thought,' Professor Wüst said. 'We need to focus the men on the spiritual dimensions of bat-tle. Perhaps we could mention Krishna's injunction to Arjuna to kill his kin, and his assurance that Arjuna would in no way do any damage to his higher self in carrying out this sacred duty.'

I already knew who Krishna and Arjuna were; like me, they were vegetarians.

My Master mused on this. 'I think we may even be bold and compare the Führer to Krishna. Our leader, too, arose at the time of his country's greatest distress, when we Germans could not see a way out. He is the reincarnation of one of those great figures of light. A line came to me in my sleep last night, and I would like to use it somehow – the one who merges with the Führer frees himself from everything, and is not bound by his deeds.'

'That's very good,' Professor Wüst said. 'One issue, however, that has been concerning me is how we explain to the uninformed that the inspiration we take from ancient India, and Hinduism, goes all the way back to the Aryan conquerors who invaded that country thousands of years ago, who inspire us through their example, and with whom I believe our Germanic peoples share a spiritual heritage.'

This seemed to irritate my Master, and he raised his voice. 'That is why I am working so hard on transforming this castle into a private sanctuary, a spiritual retreat for the highest leaders among us! If we can educate them properly in our ideology, they, in turn, will educate their subordinates.'

I growled at Professor Wüst. I did not like him. I had seen him secretly eating meat at mealtimes when my Master wasn't watching.

'If our Führer is Krishna, do you know what that makes you?' Professor Wüst said with reverence. 'You are Arjuna, the greatest warrior of all the lands.'

'I am Arjuna,' my Master said, smiling, and again, more loudly, 'I am Arjuna.' A hundred eerie voices repeated his words, reverberating around the crypt.

'Shall I read to you now?' Professor Wüst said to my Master. 'I have a parable from the ancient Chinese sage Zhuangzi that I would like to share.'

This was part of their ritual. At the end of each session, my Master lay flat on his back on the floor in what Professor Wüst called 'corpse pose', while the Professor read aloud to him.

'Lie back, close your eyes, let the words infuse your being so that you may take the highest wisdom from them,' Professor Wüst said. 'Breathe deeply, in and out, in and out.' He waited until my Master was still except for his chest rising with each breath, then he began to read:

> Count Wenhui's cook was busy dismembering an ox. Every stroke of his hand, every lift of his shoulders, every kick of his foot, every thrust with his knee, every hiss of cleaving meat, every whiz of the cleaver, everything was in utter harmony – formally structured like a dance in the mulberry grove, euphonious like the tones of Jingshou.
>
> 'Well done!' exclaimed the count. 'This is craftsmanship indeed.'
>
> 'Your servant,' replied the cook, 'has devoted himself to Dao. This is better than craftsmanship. When I first began to dismember oxen, I saw before me the entire ox. After three years' practice, I no longer saw the entire animal. And now I work with my spirit, not my eyes. When my senses caution me to stop, but my spirit urges me on, I find my support in the eternal principles. I follow the openings and hollows, which, according to the natural state of the animal, must be where they are. I do not try to cut through the bones of the joints, let alone the large bones.
>
> 'A good cook exchanges his cleaver for a new one once a year, because he uses it to cut. An ordinary cook exchanges

it for a new one every month, because he uses it to hack. But I have been handling this cleaver for nineteen years, and even though I have dismembered many thousands of oxen, its edge is as keen as though it came fresh from the whetstone. There are always spaces between the joints, and since the edge of the cleaver is very thin, it is only necessary to insert it in such a space. Thus the gap is enlarged, and the blade finds enough places to do its work.

'Nevertheless, when I come across a tough part, where the blade encounters an obstacle, I proceed with caution. First, I fix my eye on it. I hold back my hand. Gently I apply the blade until that part yields with a muffled sound like lumps of earth sinking to the ground. Then I withdraw my cleaver, rise, look around, and stand still, until I finally dry my cleaver with satisfaction and lay it carefully aside.'

'Well spoken!' cried the count. 'By the words of this cook I have learned how I must look after my life.'

That was the end of the parable that Professor Wüst read to my Master that day. I tried to think through what it might mean. It reminded me of something I had heard my Master say to his masseur once, while Herr Kersten was pounding the backs of his legs: 'Herr Kersten, what do oppressed people learn from being oppressed? Do they learn compassion, kindness or empathy, a desire to prevent suffering in others? No! They learn only this: next time, get a bigger stick.'

It is difficult for me to tell of my exile from my Master, though I deserved to be punished for my unfaithfulness.

I had been unwell, and stayed alone in my Master's office in front of the fire while he walked in the woods outside.

A strange man entered the office and I felt immediate rage that he should dare to enter my Master's domain with such nonchalance. I warned him with a growl, and when he did not back away I jumped up at him, knocking him over, and framed his neck with my teeth. I could sense his neck artery pulsing, and if he had so much as twitched I would have pierced it.

But he lay on the floor for a long time without moving, until my adrenaline ebbed and I became aware of his subservience. When I opened my mouth slightly, still keeping my teeth close to his neck, he began to talk to me in a gentle voice, saying he was sorry he had upset me and that he respected my authority.

His voice was so soothing that it began to feel like an effort not to lie down beside him, which I did, and I let him stroke my back because he knew how to move his hand firmly in the direction of my fur growth, which I liked, and in my treacherous heart I thought of how my Master sometimes stroked me in the wrong direction. I was in such a trance that I did not notice my Master had returned.

He immediately realised my betrayal. 'What have you done to my dog?' he said, very quietly.

The stranger sat up. 'I am the veterinarian you sent for to tend to your dog, the one who is sick,' he said. 'He tried to attack me. I had to calm him down.'

I went to my Master's side but he would not touch me. 'You have deprived me of the only creature who is truly faithful to me!' he said to the stranger. 'You have taken my companion away!'

The stranger was looking with fear at my Master, not understanding.

'Arrest him!' my Master shouted to one of his guards.

I tried to lick my Master's hand but he was inconsolable, and ordered that I be taken away and never allowed to return. In disgrace, I was dragged outside the compound's gates by another guard.

How could I have been susceptible to the petty attentions of a human so much less worthy than my Master? With great shame, I ran into the woods and kept running all day and long into the evening, until my exhaustion eased my despair enough to let me fall asleep.

That night, the first snow of winter fell. I woke to find my coat dusted white beneath a beech bent sideways by decades of strong winds, snow silted along its motionless branches. All around were trees so old I could sense their profound lack of interest in the fleeting lives of other creatures.

I started to sniff around, hoping to catch the scent of some plant or another to eat, and noticed tracks on the snow leading deeper into an oak grove, tracks that looked like those of a deer. I tried to ignore them. I had attracted enough bad karma; I couldn't go back to eating meat. As I watched, new tracks were imprinted in the snow, looping around the nearest oak and out towards the beech again. Something spoke right in front of me.

'Look more closely,' it said. 'You can see me if you try.'

'What are you? I can see nothing!'

'Have you forgotten that it is your birthright to see the souls of the dead?'

'Please stop!' I cried. 'I cannot bear this!'

The voice was silent for a while. I could not move for fear, but those disembodied words recalled to me something I had once known. In the evenings, my Master had read aloud to me from a book of ancient Germanic folklore. A long time ago, when the great Hermann was in power, it was believed that dogs could see the souls of the dead in these forests. When a dog seemed to be howling at nothing, it meant a soul had approached.

I concentrated on the empty air above the closest set of tracks, and finally I saw an apparition so thin, so without substance, that it could have been powder blown from a branch.

'What are you?' I asked again.

'I am the soul of an auroch,' it said.

Its bovine silver form was becoming clearer. 'What is an auroch?'

'The true aurochs were wild ox-like creatures who lived in these woods until they were hunted to extinction a few centuries ago.'

'Has your soul been here for that long?'

'No,' the creature replied. 'My kind was created more recently by the Master of the German Forests, Herr Göring. He wished to repopulate these woods with aurochs so that the German people could know what the forests looked like long ago. His scientists crossed many types of deer and oxen. But not one of us survived in the wild.'

I thought then of my grandfather caught behind the mongrel bitch, of the shame he had been made to feel. 'Why are you still here?' I asked. 'Why haven't you been reincarnated?'

'My life mate is dying. He is the last of us. I have come to accompany his soul.'

'Where is he?'

'If I told you, you would hunt and eat him,' the auroch said. 'I want him to die in peace.'

I didn't explain to the auroch soul that I was a vegetarian. I let her pass by me and on through the snow between the dark trunks.

A day passed, and another night, and still I could find no living plants beneath the snow to ease my hunger. I ate some bark and it did nothing but make the gnawing pains worse.

Late in the day, at a distance, I saw a young fox crossing a river that had frozen solid, repeatedly laying its ear against the ice to listen to the water flowing beneath.

The last thing I remembered was admiring the gracefulness of the gesture. When I returned to myself, I realised with horror that I had made a meal of the fox in a frenzy, not only breaking my Master's taboo on eating meat, but disrespecting the human law against using dogs in the fox chase. My karma was polluted again. I had perhaps destroyed forever my chance at being reincarnated as a human being.

That night I slept beneath a pine and dreamed I was curled up on my Master's lap, small enough to fit across his thighs. My dream turned sinister. A thunderbolt was aimed at me from the sky, a weapon sent by the Aryan gods to kill me. I woke up shivering in the dark, remembering my Master's love of thunderstorms, his belief that bolts of lightning were gifts of power from these ancient gods.

In the morning, the forest's silence unnerved me. When I saw a new set of ghostly hoof prints appearing in the snow, I was half glad for the company. I could just make out the outline of a pig against the evergreens.

'Hello,' I said.

'Good morning,' the pig replied. 'I wasn't sure if you could see me.'

'It is a new ability.'

'Ah,' said the pig.

'Tell me, pig, how did you die?' I asked.

'That's a personal question,' the pig said.

'Then at least tell me why you haven't yet been reincarnated.'

The pig soul stared at me, then burst out laughing.

'I'm serious,' I said indignantly. 'Don't you know about karma and reincarnation, that if you live a good, clean, brave life you will come back as a higher creature, even as a human?'

'I don't know who has been telling you these things,' the pig soul said. 'But you've got it all wrong. I don't think it works like that.'

'My Master taught me everything I know. He is inspired by ancient India, and Hinduism, and . . . he's a vegetarian. He is the reincarnation of the warrior Arjuna, and the Aryan gods of light. He has the greatest mercy and compassion for animals. I haven't got it wrong, I assure you.'

'My goodness me,' the pig said. 'He's certainly covering his behind, isn't he? Is he a follower of Zen and Tibetan Buddhism too?'

'Well, yes, I think so,' I said. 'Of course he is.'

The pig looked at me closely. 'You haven't been in the wild long, have you?' he said. 'Your paws are soft.'

'I was exiled,' I said. 'I betrayed my Master.'

'I am His Highness' dog at Kew; pray tell me, sir, whose dog are you?' the pig said.

'Pardon?' I said.

'What I'm asking is, who is your Master?'

'He is one of the leaders of this country, a great man, a gentle warrior, a protector of creatures great and small. Don't you know what he has done for you, for all animals? He has thought even of the fish in the rivers, of their suffering.'

The pig snorted. 'The suffering of the *fish?*'

'Yes. He and the other leaders have passed many laws to protect us animals. One of those laws is that water creatures can only be killed humanely.'

'Oh? And what are these humane ways of killing?'

'Fish must be stunned with a blow to the head or an electric current before being gutted,' I said. 'Eels must have their hearts cut out before they can be slit from head to tail. Crustaceans must be killed by being dropped into boiling water, not painfully brought to the boil.'

'A wise friend once told me that kindness, like cruelty, can be an expression of domination,' the pig said.

'That makes no sense,' I said scornfully.

'Look, dog, I will tell you how I died,' the pig said. 'I think it might do you good to understand how confused humans can be. They have a tendency to mix things up.'

'My Master is not to blame,' I said. 'He loved me.'

The pig cleared his throat. 'Once upon a time,' he said, 'in a village in this very forest, there lived a farmer and his wife and young children. Though they were a modern family, they were encouraged by the men who had come to power to reconnect with ancient traditions of this land. One such tradition was to adopt a pig as a family member and raise it with affection. The family chose a piglet – me – and spoiled me with treats. I was allowed inside the farmhouse, and onto the children's beds, and at night I sat with my human family in front of the fire.'

The pig soul paused. 'Are you listening?'

'Yes,' I said.

'The children grew and I grew and the farmer and his wife grew older, and one day I could no longer fit through the front door,' he continued. 'The family built a special pen for me outside, and fed me the best food scraps and visited me often. But over time, they forgot about me. The children found other things to occupy them once I was no longer a piglet. I was very lonely. I could sense that my body was changing, that my mind was not always my own – beastly impulses would surge in me, over which I had no control.

'In the middle of a hard winter, the family sold me to another farmer in the village. I was put into a stinking shed with dozens of other pigs, but I didn't know how to interact with them. Sometimes I would fly into a rage for no reason, and when the rage released me I would find the other pigs huddled warily on the opposite side of the shed.

'One night, caught in one of these mindless furies, I killed and ate two piglets. When the humans discovered what I had done, they were determined to punish me for eating my own kind. The village leader decided that this should be done in accordance with medieval law, which he believed would please the new leaders of the country who were nostalgic about the olden days. This law decreed that a human who had been sentenced to execution was to wear the skin of a pig to the scaffold, and that a pig who had eaten its own kind was to be led to the gallows wearing human clothes.

'The family who had raised me from a piglet were so ashamed of what I had done that the farmer offered his son's clothing for me to wear. The son was much older now, strong from working in his father's fields. On the day I was to be hanged, he dressed me in his own shirt and trousers. Weeping, he fastened each of the buttons along my chest, rolled up the trousers above my rear hoofs, and led me to the gallows.

'After my death, I returned to the village to watch over my family. One day humans in uniform arrived and arrested the son for breaking a law the new leaders had passed, which prohibited tormenting or mishandling an animal. They had been informed about my hanging. The son tried to explain that the villagers had thought the leaders would approve of their decision to abide by a traditional peasant law, but the men in uniform would not listen. The son was taken away, and has never returned.'

The pig soul sighed, and walked away from me. His outline grew faint in the sunlight that reached through the forest canopy. He did not say goodbye, but it seems the dead have no qualms about taking their leave without ceremony.

I was very hungry again once the ignorant pig soul had left me. I could smell something alive under the snow and I dug my claws beneath the frozen black earth, into a layer of soil that still kept some hint of mulchy warmth, until I found a giant earthworm. I recognised it immediately. It was a very rare *Lumbricus badensis*, found only in these forests, a creature my Master, in his compassion, had decreed should be protected. I had been in his office on the day he was informed that a human zoologist had cut into one of these earthworms in an experiment. A student had seen the worm move as its body was split open, and reported the incident as a violation of the new law banning vivisection. My Master had ordered that the zoologist be punished.

I ate the worm because I was starving – bad karma be damned – and lay down in the snow hoping to sleep. After a while I gave up and opened my eyes. Above me, specks of glitter were hovering in the moonlight. I focused more closely and saw a swarm of bee souls moving nimbly through the air. They made me miss my sister Blondi, who would have loved to watch them, snapping but not really wanting to catch one in her mouth.

I was too tired and sad to talk to the bee souls, but this did not stop them from speaking to me. They, too, were in mourning.

'We are grieving for our beloved von Frisch, the only human to understand the meaning of our dances, who spent his days patiently observing our patterns of movement,' they said. 'He was trying to help us survive the disease that is killing all the bees in Germany, but in the end it killed us too. The other humans in his laboratory are going to betray him. They suspect he is not one of them. His life is in grave danger.'

I closed my eyes.

'Terrible things are going to happen in these woods,' they said. 'You should leave while you can.'

For a long time – I do not know exactly how long in human terms, one year, possibly more – I lived in the woods with the souls of dead animals for company. Sometimes, when I skirted around towns and villages, I saw the souls of human beings too, but they were not interested in me, a lone dog in the wild – they were doing everything within their failing power to make themselves known to living humans, to warn them of dangers that were obscure to me.

At one stage I decided not to give up hope that I could still improve my karma, having remembered a story my Master told me of Buddha's journey towards enlightenment. Hadn't he, too, spent many years in a forest, in the wilderness, stepping over ants and caterpillars? Or perhaps it had been Krishna, or Thor, who kept vigil under a sacred fig tree? For three nights I kept watch, waiting to see the morning star rising as it did for Buddha, or Krishna, or Thor. But no star rose for me.

Much further east, I came upon great activity. I had tried as far as possible to avoid live human contact in the woods, but the smell of men's food and something else, something very familiar, drew me closer. It was the smell of my own kind: dozens of them, living alongside and protecting the brave German warriors, the men my Master commanded.

The dogs seemed to feel sorry for me in my emaciated state, and embarrassed for me that I had fallen so low. They helped me blend in, and at mealtimes some of them saved part of their own portion for me. On special occasions we were fed the same horsemeat as the humans, stringy and sweet. I watched as each horse was recorded in a logbook as having been killed by enemy fire before the men shot it themselves for food. They ground up the horse's feed into a rough flour for pancakes to accompany the boiled meat. I ate anything I was given, flesh or grain, no longer caring about karma, believing my soul to be beyond salvation.

I heard the dogs in the camp speak of Blondi often, in admiring terms. She had become quite famous by then – Queen of the Dogs, the Führer's closest companion. I wished I could see her again and bark with her in the echoing crypt at Wewelsburg, or dig at that frustratingly smooth marble star. I didn't tell them she was my sister. It did not seem fitting to drag her down with me.

I hoped beyond hope that she was as happy serving her Master as I had been serving mine. The last time I saw her at the castle, she told me something unsettling, that her Master's female companion did not like her – she had two spoiled terrier brats of her own – and took every opportunity to kick Blondi under the dining table. Blondi had resigned herself to this, for she had no way of telling her Master of this woman's coldness, her daily betrayals. Blondi had said to me she would follow her Master anywhere he asked, would endure kicks under the table until the end of her days, so long as she never had to leave his side, not even in death. And I had understood, for this was how I felt about my own Master, and still did, even after so long in exile.

One day, I was drafted into a legion of dogs who were to be given the special honour of leaving the camp to accompany the soldiers into combat. The other dogs were too busy surviving to keep an eye on me or to give me instructions, and I had no idea what to do. I ran in the wrong direction until something enormous exploded out of the ground and made me lose my hearing.

Disoriented, I ran deeper and deeper into the woods and eventually found myself in a camp of enemy soldiers. Deaf from the explosion and in shock, I had no choice but to rely on them for food until I could recover and find my way back to my own camp.

But the men fed me only once. After that, I was taken to an underground warren filled with dozens of starving dogs going mad with hunger. These dogs were chained just far enough away from one another that those who still had the energy to move could not eat their neighbours. I could feel them straining to get to my flesh as

I was led through the warren and tied up at the end of the row.

I woke in the night to find the neighbouring dog gazing at me with saliva pouring from his mouth.

The men brought water down for us, but no food. Slowly my hearing returned as my hunger expanded. Each day, the humans took one dog from the warren and attached a pouch to its back. The chosen dog was led outside, and did not return.

The dog across from me, who had seemed too weak to wish me harm or well, decided one morning to take pity on me. 'You don't know who we are, do you?' she said. 'You have not been trained.'

'No,' I said.

'When that pouch is attached to our backs, we must look for food beneath the German tanks. We have been trained to distinguish them by the smell of petrol. Our tanks smell of diesel.'

'You will find no food under their tanks,' I said. 'I know. I am German. They don't keep food there.'

'There is always food beneath the tanks,' she said.

She refused to talk to me again. Two days later, she was led out of the warren with the pouch strapped to her back.

My turn came. I was led outside. The pouch was heavier than I had imagined, and the sunlight blinding. The men pelted me with stones to make me run in the direction of my own camp.

I set my nose to the ground to try to find my way back to the Germans, to my compatriots, hoping one of them would risk everything to save me, and get the metal blight off my back. I picked up a scent leading to the west and followed it, unaware how much time I had.

But I was too weak; I could not find their camp. I collapsed beneath a tree in the wilderness. I tried to think only positive thoughts. Perhaps, just perhaps, I could still be reincarnated as a human being, as my Master had promised. Maybe the morning star – or was it the evening star? – would rise for me after all.

The pouch ticked with a metallic pulse of its own. I tried to get myself into something resembling corpse pose so that I could meditate like my Master had on the cold floor of the crypt at Wewelsburg.

I breathed in, and breathed out, and imagined that I was the legendary wolf Fenris, son of the Norse god of fire, who grew to be so strong and ferocious that the gods themselves became afraid and decided to forge a chain to restrain him. This chain was made of elements so elusive they could scarcely be said to exist: the roots of mountains, the breath of fish, the sound of a cat's footsteps. It was almost invisible, yet so strong it could keep Fenris at bay until the final battle of the gods, when the legend was that he would break free. On my back the pouch ticked. From far away, I heard my Master reciting in his hypnotic voice these words to me in front of the fire: *I am the great wolf Fenris, broken free from my chains* . . .

SOMEWHERE ALONG THE LINE THE PEARL WOULD BE HANDED TO ME

Soul of Mussel

Died 1941, United States of America

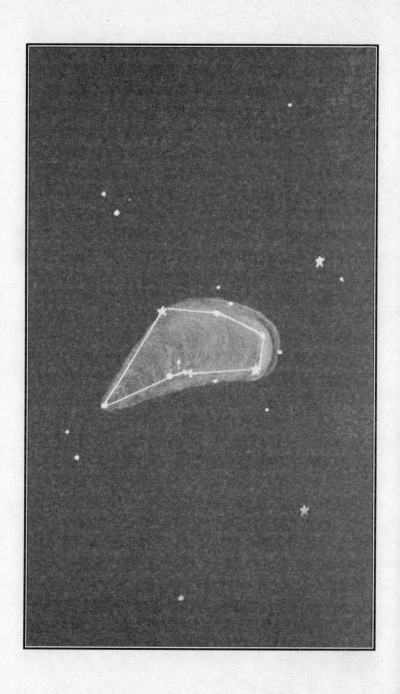

Jack loved animals (especially cats) and once wrote that when the aliens finally land on planet Earth, they will be shocked to see the way humans treat their animal brothers and sisters, 'down to the very worms yay.'

Helen Weaver, ex-lover of Jack Kerouac

I first met Muss right when I'd decided that everything was dead, when I was sick of putting down the world with theories. Muss turned up overnight in our circle with a bit of the ecstatic in him, a joyous prophet, a conman curious about everything. My friend Gallos who'd crashed on my pier in the Hudson River for a while to write his poetry, he's the one who introduced me to Muss. Story was he'd grown up poor and tough on an underwater farm out west, surrounded by crooked sad characters he loved and he hated, and somehow he'd made it to New York City all the way from the waters off Washington. Muss didn't know much, but he knew it didn't make him tick to be told from his earliest days as a juvenile blue mussel what to do, what to eat, when to secrete threads from his byssus pit, which artificial pipes to attach to and in what pattern.

Shell-crushing, sad labour of the body. He'd left behind a little girlfriend still filtering water out west but he couldn't stick around to look after her and have his spirit stolen bit by bit. He was looking – hell, we all were looking – for a new way of being, something loose, open-ended. He told us he'd hitched cross-country overland and through the Great Lakes, then on a cargo ship slipping through canals, then in cold storage, then in a bucket of seawater that kept him alive on a freight train, and finally he'd been dumped out in the Hudson, which was right where he wanted to be dumped all along.

'Wow! Man!' he kept saying the first time we talked. 'There's so many things to do and tell and feel and write and – no more fluctuating, okay, Sel, no more untrue knowledge!'

And I agreed. No more untruths.

For a while after Muss arrived, he and Gallos were connected on an invisible circuit of madman energy. Gallos memorised everything Muss said and became his disciple because he thought there was something raw and real about him and the rest of us were cooked. They had a thing where they talked fiendishly, all-day-all-night talk, six, eight, ten hours straight, trying to share everything, every single fleeting thought or twinge or appetite. I followed and listened and was interested in them because they were mad and burning with it, and they liked to have an audience for their madness. It put some method in it. Muss would visit Gallos on our pier and I would sit next to them with my shell half open, listening. They'd face each other, open their shells wide, and get down to business.

'When you moved further down the pier this morning and we passed the old mussel who told you to keep quiet, you remember,

I think there was a shoelace or something blowing in the water currents, and I wanted to tell you it reminded me of a piece of seaweed —'

'Yes, yes, of course I remember – and now you've reminded me of the thought I was having right then, about the sadness of these throwaway things and how it made my shell ache all over with —'

'But do you remember the smell in the water, fishier than normal and with a gasoline undertow to it?'

'There were industrial specks in the water, but more salt than fish. The water felt clearer at the bottom —'

'No, the light was still at the surface, murkier below . . .'

And so they would go until the sun was coming up and the night had passed, and Muss would say, 'My body is sore and hot and I want to sleep. Let's stop the machine.'

'You can't stop the machine!' Gallos would yell.

'Stop the machine,' I'd say, and then they'd be interested that I had been awake and listening to them all the night and they wanted to know how it made me feel and I would say, 'I feel that you're maniacs and I want to know what happens as you go along in the world.'

Then the smell of festy spring invaded the waters of the Hudson and we felt the sun grow warmer on our shells as we were left exposed on the piers in between tides, and I knew I had to get moving and follow my strange significant friend Muss with all his loveproblems wherever he was going across the whole damn country and see for myself the farm he grew up on, the American root of it all. And follow him further, to San Francisco and all its foggy openness. He had another girl in the Bay there and he said she'd let us move in with her and look after us a bit, let us rest our weary happy bodies until we wanted to move on again, no guilt, no bother.

I couldn't convince my girl to leave the Hudson and come with us and Muss said it was no use, that I'd find a real great girl someplace else if only I could cultivate her and make her mind my soul as he had tried and failed with every girl of his own. My girl was unhappy when I said I was off, and I thought I must be crazy, leaving her behind. But I let go of the pier I'd been clinging to for too long, put down my foot on the river floor and began to move away from her. I put a gap between us, too wide to touch across it. She turned her shell on me and went back to pumping water past her gills emotionlessly and in the underwater twilight I cursed life that it has to be so goddamned sad.

So Muss and Gallos and I, we hitched a ride on the hull of a cargo ship that Muss said would get us some ways on our journey, at least until we could drop off onto a loading dock somewhere and get picked up by a truck or train going cross-country. He said we had to hotfoot it across the middle bits or else we would dry out and die, physically and soulfully, oh yes, we would. And soon as he'd promised, we were on the road, heading west, the tarmac blurry beneath our crate, and stars, real stars, above and we knew we were alive.

Part of the ways into the big open land, we came across distant cousins of Muss's, zebra mussels who scared me stiff with their stripes and their violent, hurly-burlied way of taking what they felt was theirs for the taking. Gallos said I should be interested in them – they were *different* and different was what I was looking for, so we followed Muss to a party they told him about, a place where there'd be girls. This was freshwater territory and we knew we couldn't stay too long or else we'd be submerged and die, craving salt, but Muss needed sex the way most blue mussels need saltwater: it was holy to him and solved most everything.

We met his cousins at the exposed pipe when the tide was right and man oh man, did we get a shock that there was not an inch of space on that pipe, just zebra mussel shells packed on thick. Muss said they were halfway to covering the whole bottom of the lakes too, that there was not a single native mussel left to tell us stories. He got talking to one of the girls and that opened up some of her friends to talking to me and Gallos, until I asked about the native pearly mussels and where they'd all gone. Then the girls got bitter and closed their shells and left us to worry about their brothers turning up. I tried to explain I'd grown up in the Hudson with dream-myths about the original pearlies out west, how beautiful their shells had been, so many shapes and colours that the humans who'd first found them gave a new name to each one tugged from the watershed.

Muss came back after feeling up his zebra mussel girl and we detached from the pipe and went on our way in a box full of bait in the back of a truck, and Muss said he hoped we were heading somewhere on the West Coast. I felt the hot wind start to dry me up, and I thought about dying and all the native pearly mussel names I could remember, the ones my aunt back in the Hudson had taught me as a juvenile. Gallos got inspired and made them into a little poem. It went:

> Paper pond, squaw foot, elk toe shell
> Pimple-back, Lilliput, fat mucket shell
> Pink heel-splitter
> Purple hackle-back
> Pocketbook, snuffbox, fragile riffle shell

That was the poem. Thing that made it work was, he'd shout it out, kind of urgent-sounding: 'Paper pond, squaw foot, elk toe shell!' As if he were shouting the names of the dead.

Lucky for us, we got dumped out into the sea off the far northern West Coast. Ah to be in saltwater again, joyful salty sucking up of juices! Being on the road was good, but we weren't really ready for it, not yet; we'd only just left home, our little bodies were too soft, our minds were still forming philosophies. A boat was a better bet right then while we figured it all out, and sure enough, next thing we'd hitched a ride on a fishing vessel to Bremerton, Washington, Muss's homewaters and source of his pain and his sustenance. His old father had been on the underwater farm so long Muss told us he'd forgotten he once used to be free, that he could still be free if he only untied his threads and pushed off.

But when we got there, we couldn't find him no matter where we searched up and down the quiet hanging rows, packed thick with our brethren. Some of the elder mussels pinched their shells tight with disapproval and said to Muss his daddy had gone missing soon after Muss left, that nobody had seen him in a real long time, that he most probably had been harvested and taken up above to die. Then one of them, real crusty old bastard, said, 'You boys shouldn't be taking chances. God knows what's gonna come for you out in the deep blue. Stay put, stay here a whiles.' He leered at us, at our young flesh.

Muss got to howling about his daddy, and Gallos and I wanted out of there. So we dragged Muss with us and strayed a ways from the farm, lost and glum. It sure had taken the water out our siphons to get to the farm and find it was nothing but eerie order and rules and fear, not the root of anything. We drifted, floating, sensed the light fading and the predatory seagulls swooping above the wharves. The water beneath the dock lapped against the stinking timbers. The harbor was still and bleak. From the dimmed-out shore came a deep sigh.

And then, in the morning, we found it. The battleship. A beautiful thing, vessel of adventure, her dark shape blocking out the sunlight in the water above us, and we all felt it, a tingling promise. It was what we'd been looking for, the gorgeous chance to be tested, to leave it all behind, to join the brotherhood of those prepared to risk it all at sea. We floated closer and found a small hull-fouling young runaway community already growing on the battleship's sleek side, and we decided to hitch a ride alongside, not knowing anything except we wanted to keep getting further away from what we knew. The boys and I got set up nice and close on the toxic surface – the stuff the humans had painted on it didn't keep us off, just kept us high on fumes – and did a bit of secreting among the other stowaways, just enough so we could cling on for the journey but not get bogged down in routine.

The whole goal was detachment, gathering no algae, freewheeling. Me and Gallos and Muss, and another old friend of Muss's, Bluey, a real mild guy who'd come along with us from the farm, we would talk all the time about how we could practise non-attachment while depending for our survival on attaching to a base with our byssus threads. Bluey, he was lonely even when he was surrounded by other mussels, didn't know what was wrong with himself. He liked to watch his byssal secretions harden as they left his pit and made contact with the seawater and thought the root of all our troubles, all our sadness, was that we tried to fight the threads becoming so strong we'd never move again, tried to remain suspended in that moment of viscosity forever. He said true bliss would only come if we gave in and attached. But even Bluey knew he had to have an adventure in his halcyon days that he could feed off for the rest of his stationary life.

Muss and Gallos weren't so sure at first about hitching on a US Navy vessel, thought it was some kind of bowing down to the human establishment. As long as we were moving and moving someplace interesting, that's all I cared about. And when that battleship, that great grey tub of metal, got going on her shakedown cruise, and we felt the booming blast of the stack, and the blast of departure vibrating underwater, and the piston charges rumbling, and the giant churning of the propeller, and the water begin to move through our bodies . . . boy, did it feel good. Alackadaddy, we were on the move again!

Around us, the seascape changed as we steamed along and soon did not remind me of anything. I could take the experience into myself without it being referential and it blew my mind: each new piece of seagrass, each fish, each dot in the delicious marine snow layer of microscopic creatures so thick it sometimes blocked out the sunlight, each ocean pebble. We starved some days when the ship went so fast we couldn't trap enough tidbits, and other days we ate and ate when it slowed down, filtering and siphoning and funnelling fast as we could, and the plankton got richer and plumper the further south along the coast we moved.

The other stowaways told us things. Some of them had been at sea a long time, had a taste for hull living. One of the oldest had a bit of tragedy in his soul. He'd spent days and nights attached to a life raft along with a human shipwreck survivor, a young fellow who gave up and jumped off the raft to drown in the Carolinian sea.

This mussel said, 'You know what I learned, clinging to the life raft, feeling the heaving ocean pitching high then dropping low to reveal the sky? That the seasky is wild and beautiful as the sea itself.'

At rare moments, when the water was sugarstill, we could sense bits of the lives of the men being trained above us, in the battleship. The song of one of the cooks at sunrise: 'Everybody want to go to Heaven, but no one want to die!' The slamming pots and clattering dishes from the galley at breakfast; the throb-boom of the engines; the shouts of men playing dice on a full-moon howling night, the battleship's funnel, silhouetted against the moon, letting off clouds of blue smoke to darken the stars. Somebody on the gun crew gazing down into the dark and tremendous water of the sea, looking like he could see us all clear as day. One calm afternoon, the sea flashing green and gold, we heard the muffled shriek of a bell-whistle, the warning words: 'All hands to the boat deck. All hands to the boat deck.' Quiet followed. We waited. Our disappointment that it was nothing but make-believe: 'Drill dismissed. Drill dismissed.'

The boys and I had found a good spot on the hull in the middle of the clump of stowaways, so we had no trouble with the force of the water when it was stormy. A couple of kids at the outer edge got washed off one night when the seas were violent, and nothing we could do about it. Bluey got sad, sure, like always, and we thought about what their lives might be like wherever they landed. Maybe they would survive, catch another ride on a different hull, and who knows where that might lead them?

We lost some, we gained some. Blue mussel larvae, the real drifters, latched onto our hull at some point in our journey. One of them grew into a real beautiful girl with golden threads who Muss had a diggy thing for but she was more interested in me. We let her move in beside us, and told her what we knew about the world. 'Wow,' she said all the time. 'Wow.' And lots of glee-giggles, and next thing I thought I loved her. During our nighttime doings, Muss lay awake and listened and I was glad to let him edge in on our love wave. The girl was real nervous of spawning, and I tried to tell her it was beautiful but I lost control and it wasn't so beautiful. She sighed in the dark and I asked her, 'What do you want out of life?' which was something I used to ask all the time of girls.

'I don't know,' she said and yawned, and I wanted to cover her shell opening and tell her never to yawn, that it was not allowed, that life was too full of newness for her to be tired.

She told me her story. Survived six months as a lone larval drifter in the deepest ocean, never knew her parents. There was something different about her, couldn't figure it out at first. Then I got it: she was the first girl I'd ever known who didn't want to settle down, who I knew would leave me behind. She disappeared one day while Muss and I were arguing about the nature of reality. I got mad at him like a bullnecked idiot and we had our first real fight. Bluey sensed the shift and got sad, Gallos got jealous. Muss and I forgave each other and he made me repeat back to him: Experience is all. Right then I wanted to be inside his mind, it was that kind of hunger, something I'd never felt for a girl because a girl's mind had never grabbed me like that. I wanted to devour his thoughts. That's what I told him, and he understood.

Then some of the hitchhikers on the edge of the hull's clump started getting real nervous. They said there was a predatory dog whelk trying to invade our mussel bed and they needed our help; they had plans to tether it with threads, tie it up for good. Bluey, pacifist, refused, said it was wrong to starve another creature, even an enemy, to death like that. Muss was all for it and so was Gallos, taking his lead from Muss, and I didn't know what I felt. I thought of starving to death, what that might be like. I let Muss and Gallos go off to stalk the dog whelk with the other boys, and they had a bit of a party that side when it was done, and I woke up next to Bluey and felt the cold metal gaps on the hull where Muss and Gallos normally were and wished I'd gone with them. I couldn't understand then why I hadn't, why sometimes I liked to be alone and sometimes I wanted to be consumed by the group, at the social core of things.

Another girl came along on her fleshy foot to distract me from the miseries of myself. I persuaded her to hitch on overnight, in the spot where Muss had been. She was older than me, more ridges to her blue-black shell, and open to anything.

'You got a name?' she said.

'Sure. My friends call me Sel. But my real name is Myti.'

'A little guy like you, called Myti. That's swell.'

'Listen,' I said to her. 'You hear that?' It was the jazz music that somebody on the ship liked to play, always late at night, illicit and lovely, even underwater. 'It's the beat that gets me, like the beat of oars slapping on water.'

'Mmm,' she said.

We fooled around a bit but I was too sad to do much.

'You think that being on the same boat means something for you and your friends, don't you?' she said after a while.

'It does,' I said. 'The sea is a great leveller, a master comrade.' I closed my shell, then on second thoughts opened it again. 'It's not what you think, not really,' I said. 'I don't love it here on the hull, sometimes I hate it. I don't know whether I want to be around them all forever or run away to a dark deep valley of the ocean to be on my own.' But she was asleep.

In the morning, looking bloated with too much seawater, her gills not functioning so well anymore, she said, 'You stay hungry, boy. You're onto something, I'll give you that, living so spontaneous and all, improvising, making it up as you go. It's the only way to endure this grubby life, turn it into something sparkling. You'll get there if you can survive this. But there's no virtue in rushing towards death, remember that. Let the others live fast and die young. You live slow and die old.'

'But there are millions upon millions of mussels in the world, and I am but one,' I said.

'Yes, but you are a world in your own self, as I am,' she said. 'We are all little worlds.'

Then she moved on, to my relief, and Muss and Gallos returned yelping with glee about the dog whelk they'd tied up and left to die. Bluey stopped talking to them for a few days. He said they'd been infected by militancy and he wanted none of it. So I made a grand little speech: 'When we're sailing, man, there's no more of that stuff. We have to live together, and if we pitch in together, it's right fine. But if one guy bulls it all up, then it's no shuck-all of a trip – it'll be all fouled.' And Bluey listened, and Muss and Gallos listened.

We got to the port at Astoria, Oregon, real beautiful place, and some of the other stowaways dropped off as our battleship slowed down, soon as the smoke out of her funnels thinned. Our ship moored there awhile. For weeks the boys and I thrived and jived and got up to mischief in the bay, making sure we didn't stray too far from the hull. All of us except Bluey, who got dark and homesick there in Oregon and said he wanted to go back home to the underwater farm. I tried to talk him out of it, so did Gallos, so did Muss, but Bluey wouldn't listen. He said he missed sharing his food with his parents and his little sister and he missed having something to hold onto and knowing he could hold onto it for good. We didn't understand but we let him go, hurting, as the flames of a hot red morning played upon the masts of fishing smacks and danced in the blue wavelets beneath the barnacled docks . . .

It was not enough. I got fidgety, jumpy, I needed to feel the current through me, I needed to be on the move. Two days after Bluey dropped off to head home we felt the humans above us begin the frenetic activity which meant we would be underway again, thank the gods, and soon we felt our battleship begin to move, much more slowly than before. It was being towed across the North Pacific, south and west. Muss and Gallos and I moped about this awhile. Our fever dream all along had been to get to San Francisco Bay and hang there with his girl. I said something stupid then, that I wouldn't mind dying so long as it was in San Francisco, sunk at the bottom of a garlicky soup in a jazz club in the Tenderloin, but Muss said I shouldn't think of death like that, there was no glory in it. Only nothingness.

He and Gallos and I talked for a long time about that nothingness. Muss said we go a different colour when we're cooked, bright orange and ink-black, and I believed him but Gallos didn't. Muss said no humans will eat our byssal threads, that they don't consider them to be part of our bodies, though we consider them to be the nub of who we are. Gallos said if we ever found ourselves in a pot of boiling water we should try to keep our shells closed tight as tiddlywinks. He said it was the only way to fool the humans into not eating us. I didn't say what I thought then, what a whole fat lot of use that would be. If your game's up, it's up.

After a few weeks of towing, our battleship slowed down even more. The water got a lot saltier, the temperature rose, and we sensed that the ship was entering another harbor, on a purple coastline. Our ship put down anchor alongside a row of battleships: beautiful, untested, vulnerable, like us.

Muss detached and took a float around the underwater scene straight away and returned out of his mind with excitement. 'You know where we are?' he said. 'We're in Hawaii, my friends, y'ear me? Damn! Here we are in Battleship Row, Pearl Harbor, Hawaii, boys! We're making it!'

Then something weird happened. The temperature and salinity change acted as a stimulus to a mass joyous spontaneous spawning by every mussel in our stowaway colony on the ship's hull, every single one of us. Each male spewed sperm into the water, and each female released millions of eggs, and for days the boys and I could concentrate on nothing but fertilising, having our merry carnal way with anyone we pleased. We humped and spawned and reproduced at rates that shocked even randy little Muss. The smell of sex was almost as strong as the smell of food – there was food everywhere in the harbor, so much that we all got fat, quick and fast, fatter and fatter. I wasn't so sure this was what we'd been searching for, this life of plenty. But it felt pretty damn good, damn damn damn good, gorging and humping ad infinitum.

After a while, the sea got thick with our free-swimming drifting larval kids and started to look kind of milky. We weren't expected to care for our thousands of offspring at first. There were too many of them. But after a couple months of fornicating and feasting, the drifters we'd created began to settle down as juveniles in the open water compartments and along the pipeworks in the harbor, and against the hulls of the battleships, 'til every goddamn underwater surface had a purplish tinge to it.

And it dawned on me and Muss and Gallos what we had done. We'd wasted our freedom. We had become the elders within the colony, all of a sudden expected to be the Founding Fucking Fathers. These juveniles kept coming up to us and asking very solemnly about the *search for meaning*. What meaning? All we ever promised was a search, a journey, a trip, a ride. How did it happen, how could we possibly have spawned this strange new young beatific generation who thought that life should have *meaning*?

Gallos had a nervous breakdown, left our hull and moved in with a more radical colony to jolt himself out of his lethargy. It didn't work. He put on more and more weight, his foot got so fat and heavy he could hardly move. We had to go visit him if we wanted to see him, but we stopped going after a while because his mind had turned incurious, reactionary. He stopped writing poetry.

Then Muss and I met the lobster. He scared us at first, we thought our time was up. He looked hungry. But when we got to talking I understood he was on a journey too, not going anyplace specific, not looking for meaning, just hungry for experience, as we had been before the mistake of our communal spawning. He'd come a long way, been around the world, survived all kinds of voyages and been tossed over the side in Pearl Harbor by some humans on a trawler. The reason he didn't eat us was because he was fasting, to think more clearly.

'This European war will brew and spilleth over even here, my little *Mytilus galloprovincialis* friends, mightily galloping away from your provincial existence, so be careful,' he said. 'You'll be in demand whenever meat rationing kicks in, just you wait – you'll be famous, on menus in seedy neon-tubed diners across the country! So will I, for that matter.'

'That's not us, man,' I said. 'We're *Mytilus edulis*.'

'Oh. What a pity,' the lobster said.

On a very bright, spring-like underwater morning, he gave me and Muss each a speck of something to ingest that he said would help us see beyond the here and now. I filtered it through my body, and waited.

That speck kicked in and took me on a trip so technocolourful I hallucinated I was stuck inside an oil-slick rainbow. Muss got talkative and I went quiet. He and the lobster riffed on all sorts of things while we tripped. I heard bits and pieces as I zoned in and out, chasing the colour spectrum to the edges of the universe and back.

'No, it's the imbalance of trade,' the lobster was saying. 'The only thing the Europeans can export to America anymore is their philosophy. Existentialism. I stalked Sartre for a while. He thought he was going insane, thought he was imagining he was being stalked by a lobster! I wanted to learn from him. I wanted him to put a leash around my neck and take me for a walk, just as – if Apollinaire is to be believed – my great-grandfather was taken for strolls down the grand boulevards of Paris.'

The next time I tuned in, Muss was saying to the lobster, 'I'm a sessile species.'

'Sessile species, special specious, Seychelles series, seashell spacious,' said the stoned lobster. 'It's poetry, man. You little guys are way ahead of your time.'

We were so high we laughed hard when a starfish edged into our territory, ready for a meal of mussel. Its shape was just so out there. Five-pronged crazy joke of a creature! It got pretty close but at the last moment the lobster scared it away. Then he gave me and Muss another speck and my trip lost all colour and sank into shades of black and white and grey. Muss lowered himself onto my wavelength of silence and the lobster began to sing something sad and French. The peals of the church bells from a cathedral somewhere on shore were absorbed into the sea and drifted down to us like silver balls filled with air. It was Sunday morning.

Something splashed into the water and streaked towards us, glittering like a school of barracuda on the hunt. We admired it, not quite knowing what it was, until it hit our battleship. A living waterspout was sucked up and over the ship's stack. The lobster was killed instantly. The piece of the hull Muss and I were attached to was blasted out into the port as our ship began to list and shudder, hit again and again and again. The humans pulled alarms – no more training drills, not now – and suddenly around us in the water were things that should never be seen in the sea: valves, legs, fittings, heads, coins, arms, helmets.

We should have embraced it, this moment of collapse we had been awaiting, but we were freaking out. A man with no legs tried to cling onto our piece of the hull. Vibrations came through the water, sick wave after wave, bombs detonating somewhere in the fire, compressing my sad little sac of a body so forcefully I thought I would implode. The seawater around us began to heat up from the raging oil fires on the surface and I remembered what Gallos had said about surviving in boiling water and tried to close my shell. I couldn't. Half of it was gone.

Muss and I both knew what he had to do if he wanted to live: let go, drop off and seek shelter among the cooler beds of our kind below, leave me with my broken shell to simmer slowly in the warming water.

He landed on the seabed far beneath, nestled in among the traumatised useless colony we had created. Panic filled me; I did some deep filtering to calm down. I floated and drifted and found myself thinking of a sunset over the Hudson River way back home. I used to watch the sinking red sun from my place on the broken-down pier when the tide left me uncovered, and in the face of that terrible beauty I'd thought, Nobody knows what's going to happen to anybody besides the forlorn rags of growing old. But the panic rose again: this isn't the way it was meant to be, me, hunter-gatherer of all experience, dying at sea! What would Muss be without my gaze on him, what would any of you be? The world is upside down. Good luck with it all, the spawning, the living, the dying. I won't miss it, not much anyways.

And I thought of Muss, and thought of Muss, and I thought of Muss until I died.

PLAUTUS: A MEMOIR OF MY YEARS ON EARTH AND LAST DAYS IN SPACE

Soul of Tortoise

Died 1968, Space

1. The Hermitage

One morning in the early spring of 1913, soon after I had woken from my long winter sleep, I decided to run away from the hermit Oleg and present myself to the Tolstoy family who lived next door.

So off I set, at a rip-roaring pace, to march through the under-growth towards their estate, and three months later, in June, I reached the steps leading up to the house. I was exhausted, and could not find it in me to climb the stairs. I ate some dandelions to restore my strength and settled down to wait there, hoping that the great writer, Count Leo Tolstoy, would stumble upon me and be persuaded by my beauty – this was back in my early middle age, you see, and my shell was still a magnificent shade of topaz – to make me his pet.

Some regrets presented themselves to me while I waited, at having abandoned Oleg in his custom-built house at the bottom of the landscaped gardens of the noble family next door. The family had hired him half a century before to be their ornamental hermit in the Hermitage, one of several architectural follies the estate contained, imitations of the grand English manors of the eighteenth century. They believed him to be an old man when they appointed him, but in fact he was only thirty years old – he'd managed to fool them with his filthy long hair and beard and the druid costume he wore at their first meeting. The terms of his contract were that he would not wash or cut his hair or nails; would not engage in conversation with anybody else on the estate (servants included) except by repeating a single phrase in Latin (*Vir sapit qui pauca loquitur*: It is a wise man who speaks little); and would take exercise around the grounds whenever they had guests, looking appropriately melancholy and carrying with him a skull, a book and an hourglass which they'd purchased for him.

In return, he would receive food and wine and free lodging in the Hermitage. Fifty years later and the poor man was still there, eighty years old and completely insane. The irony of the situation did not seem evident to the family: their ornamental hermit had morphed over his lifetime into the real thing. They were always threatening to kick him out of the Hermitage (one of the granddaughters wanted to convert it to a conservatory) and replace him with a stone garden gnome, a threat to which he would respond, as per his contract, '*Vir sapit qui pauca loquitur.*'

Unfortunately he wasn't so wise in private. Over the years, he coped with his solitude by reading and talking endlessly to me. His reading was haphazard, arbitrary, manic, which meant that he burned through fascination after fascination without ever letting the knowledge he was acquiring really *change* him. Quite early on he became obsessed with the Ancient Greeks and Romans – one of his recurring delusions was that he was the original hermit owned by the Roman Emperor Hadrian. It was at this time that he named me Plautus the Tortoise, after the Roman comic playwright who valued imagination and the fantastic above anything he could scavenge from real life. Oleg built himself a lyre, thankfully using an old tortoise shell that he found in the garden, and liked to pretend he was Orpheus, entrancing me – the wild beast – with the sweetness of his playing. In this role I was expected to sway on my four feet and close my eyes.

He was won over by the scholars who argued that the famous Ancient Greek storyteller Aesop was in fact an Ethiopian slave whose fables about animals were adaptations of tales from African oral traditions, and were intended as disguised moral kicks in the teeth to his owners. Oleg would put coal dust on his face and shorten his tunic so that it looked a bit Greek, and sitting beside the fire he would orate Aesop's tales about me, the tortoise, throwing his shadow dramatically with sweeps of his arms. In this way I learned that I was given a shell because one of my ancestors couldn't be bothered going to Zeus's wedding supper and had a night in at home instead, so Zeus punished him by forcing him to carry his home on his back forevermore; and that eagles like to drop tortoises from great heights (then eat our exposed flesh) because one of my less cautious ancient ancestors insisted that the eagle teach him to fly.

Then there was Oleg's Far Eastern phase. I awoke from my

slumber one year to find that he had woven his beard into a thin plait and had broken apart the lyre so that he could use the tortoise shell for the ancient Chinese art of divining the future. This involved polishing the shell and heating it with hot pokers until it cracked. The goal for Oleg was to have his questions about the future answered in accordance with the sound, speed or shape of the cracks, but he must have done something wrong for the whole shell split in two. I watched this warily, knowing that my own attached shell stood between Oleg and his second chance at predicting the future. Luckily for me, soon afterwards he read a passage about the ancient Chinese belief that the entire universe is supported on the back of a tortoise, and he looked at me with new admiration. Not only that, but according to the Chinese, the tortoise was one of the divine animals beside P'an Ku (the Chinese version of Adam, as Oleg described him to me) while he tinkered away building the world, creating massive chunks of granite to float suspended in space.

After that phase ended, Oleg became entranced with Darwin. He declared that I was not some lowly Russian tortoise but a living fossil, most ancient of all the living land reptiles, proof that animal life had started in water and moved onto land; my kind had evolved a domed shell over the eons so that predators would struggle to get their jaws around it, the shell eventually fusing with our very backbones, while we withdrew deeper and deeper within our armour to survive. This pleased Oleg as a metaphor for his own life. He read out long passages from Darwin's notes on his expeditions, about walking for miles on the shells of live giant tortoises in the Galapagos, not once having to touch the ground for the creatures were so plentiful.

Oleg had never been a religious hermit in the true sense of the word, but a couple of years before I ran away he began to flirt with Christianity. He couldn't help but take everything literally, for during his lifetime as a hermit he'd had nobody else but me to filter his ideas through, no other human mind to help clarify his thoughts like butter, leaving them richer. So you can imagine how difficult things became for me when he read Leviticus 11:29 (*These also shall be unclean unto you among the creeping things that creep upon the earth; the weasel, and the mouse, and the tortoise after his kind*) and discovered that in early Christian art the tortoise was meant to symbolise ignorance and evil; that my slow, laborious movement across the stone floor of the Hermitage was due to the massive burden of sin I carried on my back. After surviving his first summer as a Christian, I couldn't wait to get back into my hibernation burrow and go to sleep, but when I emerged again at the end of winter, there he was, still engrossed in the Bible. That's when I decided I needed to get myself over to the Tolstoys.

2. Her Woman Friday

I was too late to become the great Tolstoy's pet tortoise. When somebody finally noticed me at the bottom of the steps and I was brought inside the house and fed a bowl of milk and bread, I was disappointed to discover he had died almost three years before.

His youngest daughter, Countess Alexandra, who had for years been his assistant and secretary, had taken to her bed to grieve after his death, and had hardly moved from there since. Her mother, Sophia, decided I should be given to Alexandra to cheer her up, and a servant was ordered to create a terrarium for me so that I could be kept in Alexandra's bedroom. It was a thoughtfully created living space, with a water bath, a hideaway for me to sleep in at night, a sandy corner, and a stone sunbathing spot that was in just the right place to catch the sunlight as it came through the windows in the morning. The maid kept the terrarium scrupulously clean, replaced the fine-grained river sand often, and on overcast days brought me a hot water bottle made of calfskin to warm up my blood.

Alexandra did not pay me much attention at first. She did nothing but read all day in bed. She sent her maid away whenever she arrived to groom her, and for the entire summer did not once wash, cut or brush her fair hair. I watched all this from my terrarium, and observed that every seven days her hair cleaned itself, quite miraculously – the oil at her scalp waxed then waned. She had her father's pointy elfin ears, and they poked out from between her fallen-forward hair when she was particularly engrossed in a book. She was very thin, and ate almost nothing. When she squatted over the chamber pot I saw that her legs too were covered with fine blonde hair.

You may think that I was dismayed at finding myself in the presence of another hermit, but to me her female solitude was so radically different from Oleg's that I was nothing but fascinated. Until I met Countess Alexandra, I hadn't given much thought to my own gender. In fact, for the decades I'd lived with Oleg he'd believed me to be male (tortoise gender is notoriously difficult to decipher), a misconception I'd encouraged for my own amusement by periodically mounting a large rock warmed up by the sun, pretending to believe it was a female tortoise. This had always seemed to make Oleg feel better about his own lack of carnal options.

It took me many days of observing Alexandra to try to understand this difference in the quality of her solitude, and the best I could come up with was that hers was a political solitude, but I didn't yet know how. She suffered from it, certainly, but not in the same way that Oleg had suffered; his state struck me in comparison as isolation, loneliness. But solitude is different, and female solitude, when it is truly chosen, can be blissful.

Alexandra's visitors – for there were many who wanted the privilege of her company – were turned away, told that she was still unwell, weak; they left her flowers or fresh mushrooms and whispered in an anxious way about her extreme melancholia, but there was nothing sickly about the way she read during those years in bed: she was beyond voracious, a famished reader. Whenever the maid announced a new batch of hopeful visitors, I could see Alexandra struggle with a vestigial impulse to give her energy – all of it, mental, emotional, physical – to her friends and family, as she must have done for the previous years of her existence. Her guilt at telling the maid to make excuses rose in her sharply once the door was closed (I could see her cheeks go pink with it), then this would give way to relief that she could safeguard her energy, her mindful wanderings, for just a little longer.

I wanted to know, more than anything, what it was she was reading with such intensity, what answers she was seeking. One morning in autumn, when the maid had taken the terrarium out of the bedroom for cleaning and left me sunning myself on the floorboards, I decided to climb up to Alexandra and her books on the bed. I have the advantage of being small – the Russian tortoise is one of the smaller varieties, hence our popularity as pets – and a surprisingly good climber, and soon I had pulled myself up onto the bedspread and was stalking in my mechanical way across the quilt towards her. She looked up at the movement and – to her credit – did not jump at finding a small reptile sharing her bed. She simply watched my journey, and when I made it all the way to the pile of books I put my front legs with some effort on top of them and stuck my head out as far as I could to read the titles.

At this she laughed, made a little warm space for me against the pillows, and began to read aloud. We didn't stop reading even when her meals arrived on a tray. While she read, I ate what I could of her lunch and dinner to thwart her mother, who came after every meal to check if Alexandra had eaten. I knew it was bad for my liver to ingest so much cream and meat, but I didn't care. I crouched beside her and watched the sun cross the bedspread and listened to her voice, breathed in her smell of blackcurrants and salt, yeast and orange peel. I had to concentrate hard to hear her – hearing isn't my strong suit, but my sight and smell tell me most of what I need to know – and this is how I became acquainted with the writings of the early American feminist Elizabeth Cady Stanton, and with Alexandra's reasons for choosing a period of solitude.

I am aware that one person's insights and epiphanies from unique reading journeys are not always interesting to another, just as other people's tales about their travels mostly inspire boredom. I've wondered why this is for humans, and I've decided it has something to do with the perceived alchemical magic of the discoveries that books (or travel) enable: they are utterly private and idiosyncratic, and, to the person undergoing them, feel ordained, auspicious, designed especially for them at that particular moment in their lives. In a century during which many people have lost the religious framework of fatalism, it seems books have become signs to interpret and follow – this book has come into my life for a reason, the author is speaking to me and to me alone. And this, in a strange way, leads to people becoming evangelical about books. You *must* read this, they preach, forgetting that it was the way they stumbled serendipitously upon the book – finding it abandoned on the seat of a coach, or dusty in the attic, or neglected in a dark stack at the library – that was partially responsible for its powers.

But in the days when reading aloud was the norm, this magic was shared. The words Alexandra read electrified us both, none more so than this moving passage from Elizabeth Cady Stanton's speech to the US House Judiciary Committee in 1892, when she was – think of it! – seventy-six, an old woman giving an address to powerful men that she dared to title 'The Solitude of Self':

> In discussing the rights of woman, we are to consider, first, what belongs to her as an individual, in a world of her own, the arbiter of her own destiny, an imaginary Robinson Crusoe with her woman Friday on a solitary island. Her rights under such circumstances are to use all her faculties for her own safety and happiness . . . To appreciate the importance of fitting every human soul for independent action, think for a moment of the immeasurable solitude of self. We come into the world alone, unlike all who have gone before us, we leave it alone, under circumstances peculiar to ourselves. No mortal ever has been, no mortal ever will be like the soul just launched on the sea of life.

Alexandra mused to me about the meaning of this. You could fool yourself your whole life and think you're not alone, but you will know – how clearly you will know – when you're in pain, when you're dying. And if a person has not been allowed, in times of solitude, to develop her mind's many resources (intellectual, creative, emotional, spiritual) to shore herself up, to provide good company for herself, she will experience the further desolation of being alienated even from her best self. Nothing could be lonelier. On a visit to the exiled Prince Kropotkin in England, an anarchist philosopher whom Alexandra's father had also admired, Elizabeth Cady Stanton asked how he'd endured his time in the prisons of Russia and France, and he responded that he'd tried to recall everything he'd ever read, and had reread it in his mind and heart, secure that nobody could invade the sovereignty of his thoughts.

For Alexandra, whose mind had been nurtured unusually, who had been exposed – thanks to her father – to ideas and varied ways of thinking, who already had robust resources of self to draw on, Elizabeth Cady Stanton's words were reassuring. Alexandra had withdrawn into solitude to test those resources, in a sense, to know her own mettle, but there was something else quite complex at work in her decision, something she explained to me between readings. Throughout his life, but especially in his older age, her father, Count Tolstoy, had swung between the two poles of engagement and detachment. Just before his death, he had once again determined to become an ascetic – to renounce all possessions, including the family's properties and the copyright to his own great literary works – and she had helped him to leave home secretly. How was she to have known he would catch pneumonia and die in the godforsaken, freezing stationmaster's home only days later?

Worse, since his passing she had been appointed the keeper of his archive, his literary and legal guardian, for her mother had made sure that her father was not able to give up his copyright. This posed to Alexandra a terrible dilemma. She thought over and over of her father's words: *I'll go somewhere where no one can bother me . . . Leave me alone . . . I must run away, run away somewhere.* Alexandra, in turn, felt she needed to retreat from the world, to lose herself in the only asceticism she could legitimately choose – the solitude of the sickly – while she decided what to do with her life. When her mother knocked on the door, she said, 'Leave me alone.' To herself she muttered, 'I must run away.'

The days shortened. I sensed that my own time of temporary withdrawal from the world was upon me. I stopped eating Alexandra's meals and felt my heart rate slow down, leaving me sluggish. I struggled to join her on the bed, and when she came to investigate she found me buried head first in sand in the murkiest corner of my terrarium. The maid had a hibernation box built for for me, layered with moist pumice, soil and peat moss. As soon as Alexandra placed me on top of the moss, I was possessed with the urge to dig down until I was covered and give in to the most rapturous sleepiness. She watched me burrow into oblivion, I imagine, with envy.

In March I awoke and was reinstated in Alexandra's room. I was dazed and groggy, and it took me about a month to find my bearings and feel hungry again, to really pay attention to my surroundings. Alexandra was solicitous – she bathed me to loosen a winter's worth of dirt from my body, clipped my claws, and rubbed hoof oil into my shell to make it glister. But something was wrong. I basked in the sun, stretched out flat on the floor with my head, limbs, tail all as far out of my shell as possible, and pretended to close my eyes so that I could spy on her.

The first warning sign was her hair – so clean it kept wisping out of her French braid, which itself warranted some staring. I'd never seen her hair arranged before. Then there was her smell, which had changed to the point where I almost didn't recognise her at first, due to the soap and perfume she was using: not bad odours, but they interfered with my ability to pick up her body's scent signature. But the most obvious sign was that Alexandra no longer spent her days in bed. The windows were thrown open, the bed was made, and instead of reading books, she read long letters greedily and secretly (not reading them aloud even to me) and wrote longer replies. She encouraged me to spend time outside every day, and tried to teach me to return to her by playing the lowest note on the piano.

If I'd had the slightest doubt that her time of hibernation was over, that doubt was banished when she took me into the garden for a picnic lunch attended by dozens of her friends. The outside tables were laden with food, and she had asked the maid to put together a private feast for me: chickweed, clover, sow-thistles, goat dung, buttercups, raspberries, crushed snails, cucumber, cress. I looked up midway through my massive meal and was stunned to see Alexandra had eaten her way through an entire cherry cake and was starting on a savoury dill tart. Sitting beside her, watching her eating with gusto, was a young man in uniform who could not hide his adoration, and I knew in that instant that he was the author of the letters she had been devouring in her room. She looked at him and smiled, and he wiped a pastry crumb from her bottom lip, and I could see then that she had found her appetite again, for all sorts of things.

Later I came to understand that he was part of it, certainly, but not the whole. It was through him that she had been reawakened to her father's commitment to helping those in need, and to the

twin callings of a true hermitess, for whom solitude and contempla-
tion must lead, in the end, to engagement. War had been declared,
and Alexandra knew what she needed to do in order to emulate her
father's devotion to social reform, nonviolence, simplicity and service. Before the summer was over, Countess Alexandra had eloped
with her lover, and when he was sent to the front, she threw herself
into her work in the hospitals for wounded and dying soldiers with
a passion of which her father would have been proud.

Without any bitterness on my behalf, she left me to live a comfortable decade and a half in the Tolstoy family home, cared for by
the maid, skipping out on half of the misery and joy of each year
through my hibernation. Until one day in 1929, when I awoke to
find myself in great physical pain on a ship to London, my terrarium packed up into a box addressed to one Mrs Virginia Woolf,
Bloomsbury, England.

3. A Terrarium of One's Own

Virginia Woolf, on opening the box sent from Russia containing me,
immediately sensed I was in pain and quickly figured out what to do
about it. She gave me a warm salt bath daily to treat my infected
shell, and fed me only water and fresh greens for weeks. She understood that my shell is a living and very sensitive part of my body, not
anything like the fingernails of humans, and she was horrified that
somebody had been stupid enough to carve words into it, across the
bumps and scutes. In the box I'd travelled in, she found a single clue
to my origins: a copy of Leo Tolstoy's short story 'Strider: The Story
of a Horse', in Russian.

An émigré friend of hers eventually translated it, and discovered it was not in fact Tolstoy's story told from the point of view of Strider the horse, but the prison diary of Alexandra, who had been arrested and imprisoned several times since the Russian Revolution, and had asked her husband to smuggle her diary out of the country using me as a decoy. Rolled up and tucked under my infected shell was a note from Alexandra to Virginia in English, saying how much she admired her writing and begging her to care for both me and her diary until she could escape from Russia.

Alexandra's husband – without knowing that it would hurt me – had decided to have some of the great Tolstoy's words carved into the living tissue of my shell, in the hope it would give me a degree of notoriety in London and thus ensure my survival (and that of Alexandra's diary), and in that his instinct was right. Virginia set me up in pride of place in her living room in Bloomsbury, and soon everybody she and her husband, Leonard, knew was stopping by to meet me, Tolstoy's tortoise, with the great man's reported deathbed words translated and carved on my back: *I love many things, I love all people*.

On discovering me in the box, Virginia had done what she usually did when she encountered a new phenomenon – in this case, a live tortoise – and went to the literature. She took out every book on tortoises she could find in the library, and read choice tidbits aloud to Leonard after dinner in the evening. With great good humour, he endured many monologues from her about the miracles of tortoise reproduction: how a female tortoise has absolute control over her own reproductive processes and can decide when to fertilise her egg (male sperm can survive in her body for as long as two years until she might elect to use it); if she changes her mind once the egg is fertilised, she can reabsorb it or hold off laying it until the time is right. Virginia was also greatly amused by the female tortoise's general indifference to the lovemaking exertions of the male. One of the books included a naturalist's description of a female tortoise leisurely finishing her meal of dandelions, not noticing that a male had mounted her until he hissed and squealed (for they do squeal) his way to climax.

Not many people know this, but Leonard used a pet name for Virginia in private, learned from her siblings: Goat. Virginia's nickname for her sister was Dolphin, and Virginia's close friends were secretly delighted on receiving an animal moniker from her, for it was the ultimate sign of approval. Virginia had, as a girl, tended a small menagerie of her own that contained a mouse, a marmoset and a squirrel. Her very first published piece of writing was an obituary she wrote for the family's beloved dog, and when I arrived in her life she was working intermittently on a biography of the dog Flush, a cocker spaniel owned by the nineteenth-century poetess Elizabeth Barrett. Flush had kept Elizabeth company through her years of being an invalid and accompanied her to Italy when she eloped with Robert Browning.

Virginia liked to try out pieces from the book about Flush on me, for we quickly became close. She sensed that I didn't like it when the tone veered towards the ironic, tongue-in-cheek style that humans seem to adopt automatically when writing from the perspective of an animal. It was a cheeky book, certainly, provocative even – it fit with her desire at the time to play with the conventions of traditional biography – but that didn't mean it couldn't also be moving. Virginia had some daddy issues, but similar to Alexandra's, hers were of the best possible kind (the inspirational, the aspirational), for her father had edited the

Dictionary of National Biography and he and her beautiful arty mother had always been surrounded by authors and artists. And now Virginia and Leonard were surrounded by their own most interesting contemporaries, painters and poets, and Virginia was on fire with curiosity and creativity.

I was most impressed by the passages in *Flush: A Biography* in which Virginia attempted to understand at a sensory level what it might be like for a dog to experience the world through smell. This was probably due to my own similar hierarchy of senses, with smell right at the top. She wrote the sights of Florence like no writer ever has or ever will, by imagining how they might smell to Flush the dog:

> He slept in this hot patch of sun – how sun made the stone reek! he sought that tunnel of shade – how acid shade made the stone smell! He devoured whole bunches of ripe grapes largely because of their purple smell; he chewed and spat out whatever tough relic of goat or macaroni the Italian housewife had thrown from the balcony – goat and maca-roni were raucous smells, crimson smells. He followed the swooning sweetness of incense into the violet intricacies of dark cathedrals; and, sniffing, tried to lap the gold on the window-stained tomb.

When the book was published, a few years after I arrived in London, she took me with her on her little round of public and private readings and talks. She would start off by mentioning two Russian authors she admired, the usual duo of Gogol and Tolstoy, but then she'd lighten the serious atmosphere that settled on the room when she mentioned those venerable names by asking what these two men might have in common, other than being Russian authors of proximate generations. Both of them, she would say, dared to imagine themselves into the mind of an animal; both could at one stage find no way to say what they wanted to say except by making that animal speak for them. Then she would tell the anecdote about me, her Russian tortoise – sent to her by Tolstoy's daughter, who had in fact recently escaped from Russia with her husband to settle in America – and how she often found herself wondering what stories I could tell about Tolstoy (she wasn't aware he had died before I'd joined the family). Her audience would laugh, and the scene would be set very nicely for her to read out a passage from *Flush: A Biography* without it seeming completely ridiculous; in her clever way, she had cleared a little space for herself in history, aligned herself with the greats in taking this risk. And with a glance at me – a kind of tribute, I'd like to think – she would read out my favourite paragraph of the whole book, a moment that does justice to both the poet Elizabeth and her dog Flush by showing them as equals in their inability ever to fully understand each other: not so different then, from a biographer trying to get into the skin of her subject.

As they gazed at each other each felt: Here am I – and then each felt: But how different! Hers was the pale worn face of an invalid, cut off from air, light, freedom. His was the warm ruddy face of a young animal; instinct with health and energy. Broken asunder, yet made in the same mould, could it be that each completed what was dormant in the other? She might have been – all that; and he – But no.

Between them lay the widest gulf that can separate one being from another. She spoke. He was dumb. She was woman; he was dog. Thus closely united, thus immensely divided, they gazed at each other.

Many times during my happy years with Virginia, I was grateful for the good fortune of having arrived on her doorstep and nobody else's, for this was London in the 1930s and the pet tortoise craze was in full swing. Virginia followed the travesties of the tortoise trade as they were reported in the papers: millions of us imported each year from North Africa, arriving with broken limbs and shells from being packed into crates one on top of the other; a thousand dead spur-thighed tortoises discovered in baskets on the Barking foreshore. Hardly any that survived the journey made it through their first winter in Britain. Outside schools you could buy a baby tortoise and a goldfish for sixpence, and if they both died – as was likely – you could buy another pair the next week. In any local pub, you could find pet tortoises being forced to race across the billiard tables, and given a puddle of beer to drink at the end. At the other extreme, a live tortoise forgotten by a wealthy passenger on a Paris–London flight was discovered wrapped in pink cotton wool, with emeralds and rubies cruelly encrusted in its shell.

But in Bloomsbury, during those years before the next war started, I was treated not as a mere pet, but as the worthy subject of great art and poetry. Tortoiseshell objects – hair combs, calling card boxes, the rare snuffbox – were banned in my presence, Virginia made sure of it. Tributes of poems were welcomed. More than one guest greeted me with D.H. Lawrence's words about my species:

On he goes, the little one,
Bud of the universe,
Pediment of life.

And all that time I lived with her, I watched Virginia write,
as the little dog Flush had watched Elizabeth Barrett Browning's
fingers forever crossing a white page with a straight stick, longing to
blacken the paper with his paws.

This lovely literary life with Virginia and the Bloomsbury Set
was upended by the London Blitz. I mean this quite literally. One
moment I was sunning myself in the Woolfs' drawing room, the
next I was buried in the rubble of their home after a bomb hit it
while they were out. I felt very calm for the first day I spent hidden
away in my shell in the darkness of the ruins. I thought about the
card that the Woolfs had pinned to their gatepost, offering sanctuary to any animals and their owners left without a home after a raid,
and the card pinned next to it stating that a tortoise lived in this
home and would most likely be found in the drawing room in the
event of a bomb hitting the house, so the rescue squad would know
where to look. Virginia had taken a great interest in the training of
the bomb-raid rescue-squad dogs, and I thought about them for a
while, imagined them working away above me in that purposeful
canine manner, knowing that a creature – me – was alive and waiting to be rescued from beneath the layers of debris. I knew Virginia
would be desperate for them to dig me out, that she would haunt
the site of her home until I was found, from the moment the all-
clear had sounded until the next siren began to wail.

Somehow in the bomb's violence, the parrot that lived next door
had ended up near me under the rubble, alive in its cage, saying over

and over, 'This is my night out! This is my night out! This is my night out!' until it died. I began to feel weaker. I recalled that Virginia had told Leonard the morning before about the Nazis burning Swastikas into the backs of tortoises. Tolstoy's words on my back ached a little, but I couldn't tell if it was from residual pain or fresh shell trauma.

What else did I think about while I was trapped beneath the rubble of the Woolfs' London home, waiting for a mongrel rescue dog named Beauty to dig me out? I thought of Virginia feeding me flower petals according to her mood and the emotional association that flower had accumulated over centuries: narcissus with egoism, dandelion with feelings of expansiveness, wormwood with bitterness, columbine with sadness, snapdragon with desire, water lily with indifference, and rose – of course – rose with love. I thought of her sitting with a copy of the French author Bataille's new book open on her lap, reading his anti-sentimentalist essay 'The Language of Flowers': 'For flowers do not age honestly like leaves, which lose nothing of their beauty, even after they have died; flowers wither like old and overly made-up dowagers, and they die ridiculously on stems that seemed to carry them to the clouds . . . love smells like death.'

Love smells like death, that's what I thought while I was buried in the rubble. I said my farewells to Virginia then, mourned losing her and mourned her loss of me. When she drowned herself five months later in the River Ouse, I did not mourn again. She left a note for Leonard, a love note that I'd watched her compose before she began to gather up stones from the garden of their country home in Rodmell, stones to put in her coat pockets.

4. Tortoises All the Way Down

In Virginia's will, she asked that I be given to Eric Arthur Blair, who had published his account of living as a tramp in London and Paris (a book Virginia much admired) under the pen name of George Orwell to avoid embarrassing his respectable family. She had heard he tended a small menagerie on his family's farm in Wallington, and she hoped I might be welcomed there, safe from the city bombs.

I don't have much to say about my time with George Orwell. I didn't like him, and he didn't like me. His menagerie consisted of a rooster called Henry Ford and a poodle named Marx and the two were usually locked in attempted mortal combat. I kept a low profile. During the war, his wife was away in London working in the Censorship Office, but George had been declared unfit for service due to injuries he sustained while fighting in the Spanish Civil War a few years earlier. He was principled, no doubt about it – deeply so, in fact, and one of the first to uncover and understand the evils of fascism – but that didn't make him good company.

I try now to take some pride in the fact that I observed George working on his masterpiece, *Animal Farm: A Fairy Story*, but in truth during that time I was depressed and not at all interested in what he was writing. I've heard he didn't bother to put a tortoise in the book – not even a totalitarian tortoise! – which says much about his feelings towards me. Mainly what I remember of the war and my time with George is the surprisingly delicate smell of potato blossoms. George became obsessive about planting and tending his potato patches on the farm, doing his part 'digging' for the war effort, helped by a handful of exhausted Women's Land Army girls who worked harder than any humans I've ever encountered, trying to keep the farms in the area productive in the absence of men, not stopping from five in the morning until midnight. The joke about the Land Girls was that even the cows could see how tired they were, and would jump up and down while being milked to make it easier for them. At one stage, George joined the Home Guard to train up younger men in the region, but he mishandled a mortar and quite severely wounded two of his trainees. After this he focused mainly on his potatoes and his writing, only to be told by most publishers that they couldn't publish his animal fairy story because the Soviets were an important ally, and anybody could see that the book was a not so thinly veiled critique of the rise of Stalinism in the Soviet Union.

Owning a pet tortoise seemed to strike George as a quasi-aristocratic thing to do, which he disliked, but one day after the war ended, soon after his animal fairy tale was published by a brave publisher, and his poor wife had died, he must have thought it would be invigoratingly ironic to take me along on one of his tramping expeditions to London, perhaps because of Tolstoy's words on my back. His tramping book, *Down and Out in Paris and London*, had been published many years before, the same year as Virginia's *Flush: A Biography*, but George still got the urge to go slumming quite regularly, and since his wife's death he had been a little unhinged. George always called himself Burton when he was in his tramp disguise. Burton had slummed around the poorer areas of England for years, sleeping in lodging houses, spending time out on the road and in the East End, working on hop farms in Kent, washing himself on the beach, deliberately trying to get arrested for being drunk so that he could write about spending Christmas in prison.

So on this particular day, Burton – dressed in his tramp uniform of oversized unwashed clothes, and already coughing with the tuberculosis that would kill him, a believable hacking tramp's cough – tucked me under his arm and took me to a public lecture on astronomy being given by the famous philosopher Bertrand Russell. Burton deliberately took a seat near the front, which had the effect of clearing the first two rows because of his carefully curated tramp odour. I sat on the seat beside him, embarrassed, until Mr Russell started his lecture and I fell into fascination with what he was describing: the moon orbiting the earth, our lowly earth in an orbit around the sun, and that sun itself spinning in its own orbit around the centre of the Milky Way galaxy. Smaller orbits nesting in bigger orbits nesting in enormous ones. It made my head ache with pleasure to think of it.

At the end of the lecture, during the time for questions, Burton the tramp stood and swayed a bit, as if he were drunk. The audience went stiff and quiet, and Mr Russell looked as if he were bracing himself for unpleasantness.

'None of this is true,' Burton said loudly. 'The four corners of the earth are held up by pillars on the shell of a massive tortoise!'

Mr Russell, long-suffering philosopher that he was, had clearly heard this claim before. He decided to engage rather than ignore Burton. 'Dare I ask what the tortoise is balancing on?'

'Ah, good question, verrry good,' Burton slurred purposefully. 'But it's tortoises all the way down.'

'Yes, that's what I feared,' Mr Russell said with a sigh, and dismissed the audience.

I wanted to disappear with shame. But it was thanks to Burton taking me along to hear those words about nested orbits that I first began to dream of seeing space.

I ran away from Burton/George soon after that tramping epi-
sode, and did some long years of slumming myself, taking odd gigs
and owners here and there to stay alive. For about ten years, I lived
at a wildlife park in Wiltshire where the staff painted numbers
on the shells of the resident tortoises. On Saturday mornings, the
numbers of the first three tortoises that lumbered out of our shelter
were recorded and used for the staff's weekly bet on the horses, but
apparently the famed oracular powers of tortoises leave much to be
desired, for not once did any of the selected horses win. The staff
didn't paint a number on me because of my shell engraving, from
which they wrongly assumed that my last owner had been one of
the new breed of free-loving hippies who also loved many things,
and all people. The food there was pretty decent and the other tortoises were tolerable, and I laid a few eggs, which kept me busy
until the hatchlings left. But all along I knew I had another destiny
waiting for me.

One day I heard the staff at the wildlife park discussing the
Cold War – a term I was familiar with, for good old George had
coined it years before. Then the staff members started talking about
the space race between the Soviets and the Americans: a race to
put a human being on the moon, to prove once and for all which
country was superior (and along the way to get as many spy satel-
lites into orbit as possible). This was a contest of epic proportions,
ancient in scope, really, for the spoils of victory were hugely symbolic and the humiliation for the loser was public and absolute. And
who were the first proxy astronauts for each nation, while they fran-
tically tried to make space travel safe for humans? Fruit flies and
monkeys, dogs and frogs, mice and rabbits, rats and cats. And a
guinea pig – most true to its name, used as a guinea pig.

I knew immediately I had to present myself to the Americans or the Soviets – I didn't care which – whoever would be prepared to put me in a rocket and fly me into space! With this in mind, I slowly made my way back to London and headed for the only place I thought I might find both, or at least some communists: the theatre district. Once there, I was adopted by a young British playwright named Tom Stoppard, who was working away at a play where the main character, a philosopher, accidentally kills his pet tortoise by stepping heavily on him. And all along, the philosopher's wife is watching, on television, two British astronauts land on the moon and fight about who will get the single space left on their crashed capsule to get back to earth. I interpreted this as a sign I was on the right track. Tom wasn't sure how he wanted the audience to react to the death of the tortoise – big gasps as the mechanical tortoise broke apart, or guffaws? It was still a rather confusing play at that point, not yet ready for an audience.

Tom had recognised the words on my back as being among Tolstoy's last, and he took me with him to parties to show me off. At these gatherings, I tried to ingratiate myself with anybody wearing a black turtleneck, as previous experience had shown this often meant they were either American or communist, or both. One of Tom's friends noticed this, and also noticed the intensity with which I listened to Tom experimenting aloud with his fake television scenes of men on the moon for his play-in-progress, and he did me a great favour. He asked another friend, a London-based communist about to leave on a guided tour of the USSR, to take me with him and present me to the Soviet Space Program as a gift to break the ice (Tolstoy's words on my back would either help or hinder my chances, they weren't quite sure which). Tom's friend thought the

Soviets had a better chance of getting a man on the moon – and in the interim, a tortoise – than the Americans; the Soviets had, after all, won the first heat of the race by putting Yuri Gagarin into orbit around the earth in the early spring of 1961.

5. Deedle Dum Dum

The ploy worked. The Soviets were sending animals into space like there was no tomorrow (which, for the animals, there mostly wasn't), desperate to finalise their research on the viability of manned space flight and the effects on living creatures of prolonged weightlessness and radiation from the Van Allen belts, and get a man on the moon before the Americans. They'd heard rumours that the Americans had sent a bunch of black mice into space and the cosmic rays had turned them grey; this would be undesirable in humans.

I was accepted into the Soviet Space Program and started my training in the lab of the resident space biomedical expert, Dr Yazdovsky. I found myself unexpectedly pleased to be back home among my Russian countrymen after so many years overseas, and I quickly became one of the doctor's favourite animals. He nicknamed me Bert, because Soviet intelligence had uncovered the existence of a nasty cartoon character in the US named Bert the Turtle, who campaigned for the American public to duck and cover in the event of the Soviets attempting to liquidise them with an atom bomb. I wasn't a turtle, but that wasn't the point. The nickname was really just an excuse for Dr Yazdovsky to start singing the Bert the Turtle song as loudly as he could whenever he saw me wandering about in my massive, state-of-the-art Soviet terrarium.

I thought Dr Yazdovsky's frequent serenading might increase

my chances of being sent up in a rocket, but during the early to mid-1960s he was very much focused on putting dogs in space. The Americans favoured monkeys because they could use their hands, but Dr Yazdovsky felt that small dogs would be less restless in the rocket cabin than apes; they also cost less to train, and two dogs could be sent up together without a problem, generating two comparative data sets. Female dogs were preferable, as they didn't have to lift a leg to urinate (a plus in the small cabin); mongrels were ideal since they were hardier than purebreds and could better withstand the tribulations of space flight. All of Dr Yazdovsky's dogs had white fur, to show up better on film recordings transmitted from their capsules. Most of the dogs tolerated the training well (learning to wait patiently for weeks in small compartments; being spun in a centrifuge; using special trays to get food). The only problem was that they had a habit of running away just before the scheduled takeoff, almost as if they could sense they were about to be shot out into the ether.

While I was living in the lab, one of the dogs, Smelaya, managed to escape the day before her launch and went missing in the wilds surrounding our remote research facility. Dr Yazdovsky went into a panic, not because he had lost a test-flight subject, but because he was worried she would be eaten by the packs of wolves who lived beyond the facility, whom we sometimes heard howling at the moon as if they too wanted to go there. He had a kind heart, Dr Yazdovsky, though he tried to hide it. When Smelaya returned the next day, right on time for her rocket launch, he let her lick his face, something he always told the other lab workers never to do, for it encouraged dog–human bonding. She and her co-pilot, Malyshka, were shot into low orbit, and found dead in their sealed metal container after it parachuted back to earth.

I would have liked to have known Laika, the first animal to orbit the earth. She was a stray that Dr Yazdovsky noticed lurking beside the rubbish bins outside the facility and on a whim decided to put in the cabin of *Sputnik II* when it was blasted into orbit around earth in 1957. The video recorders in the cabin revealed that she was quite happy up there, able to move a bit, bark, and eat food pellets from an automatic dispenser. For a week she orbited the earth alive. Then the oxygen in her capsule ran out and she died, but her capsule stayed in orbit for months.

I didn't get to hear much about the dogs' experiences in space because most of them were one-way passengers. The few that did make it back I spoke to whenever I had the chance. I suppose it was my early lessons in the varieties of solitude – from Oleg, from Alexandra, from Virginia, even from George – that had stayed with me; here was a chance to know what it might mean to be truly alone, in the ultimate solitude of space. I longed for the chance to experience that solitude myself.

Here is a transcript of an interview I did with a pair of dogs, Veterok and Ugolyok. They made it back alive after a space flight onboard *Kosmos 110* in 1966, after breaking the record for the number of doggy days survived in space (twenty-two) and number of earth orbits (three hundred and thirty):

What did you think about during your time up in space?

VETEROK: I was intending to think about my work – consolidate my training, plan my next approach to Dr Yazdovsky's maze, or perhaps even come up with an introduction for a pep talk to the other lab dogs on my return. But I found I could not think about anything clearly. I did very badly on the tests the lab engineers set for me up there, basic stuff. I felt restless all the time.

UGOLYOK: Yes, me too. I felt as if I had no control over the content of my thoughts. If I saw a pellet of my shit floating about in the capsule, I could think of nothing but shit for hours, even days. I began to hallucinate, to see and hear strange things – one morning I heard a choir singing and saw the sun rising above the steeple of a church. I thought a mini-rocket ship had implanted itself in my stomach and I tried to scratch it out.

VETEROK: Oh, and another thing. I thought a lot about that American monkey, Enos – you know the one in the photograph stuck on the wall in the lab, when he'd just returned from his trip into space and he looks angry as hell? I never understood that before, why he would be so furious. I knew the story, that up goes Enos in his capsule into space, and he's pulling all the correct levers to get water and banana-flavoured tablets, just like he's been trained. But there is mechanical trouble while he's up there and instead of getting sips of water or tablets, he starts getting zapped by the electric pads wired to the soles of his feet. He gets back to earth, gets out of the capsule and the NASA guys are smiling, holding his hands, but Enos is fucking *mad*. This used to make me laugh. But up in space, I just had to think about this, about Enos getting buzzed on his feet for doing the right thing – the right thing! what he's been trained to do! – and I wanted to bite somebody's face off.

Did you two get on up there?

UGOLYOK: Absolutely not. We drove each other mental, cooped up like that together. It's not natural. If Veterok touched my toy ball, I just couldn't stand it, it became a really big deal.

VETEROK: It was very stressful. We both felt as if our survival instincts were kicking in even though we knew rationally we had enough resources for us both to survive the trip. We became very selfish, childishly possessive.

Which part of the trip was the hardest, the beginning or the end?

VETEROK: It's funny, you know, but actually it was the middle that was worst for me. It's exciting at the start and the finish – lots of adrenaline, the stuff of peak experience – but in the middle it gets monotonous. And I took this out on Ugolyok but also on the crew members on the ground. They couldn't tell, of course, they didn't know why I was barking so much, but I was telling them where they could stick it, among other things. It was displaced tension from the stress of the situation we were in, but the rage I felt was very real, very justified, in the moment.

UGOLYOK: Yes, it was in the middle that we started to really irritate each other. I got a bit depressed during that time, once I'd mastered the basic tasks I'd been set by the crew on earth, to test my reactions. That's when the doubts kicked in too – about what we were doing, and why. I mean, you see the earth below you – it's just like they say, suddenly there it is, a colourful ball floating in the middle of absolutely nothing, and . . . well, I just don't know if anybody can ever recover from that. I'm still struggling to take life seriously again now that we're back down here. It seems like one big sick joke. I thought it would be liberating but — *[Veterok mutters something to cut him off]*

What advice would you give to other dogs being trained for space-flight?

VETEROK: If you go up in a pair, you must try to think of the other dog first, however hard it is. Let him drink water first, let him play with your toy ball, let him tell the same dumb joke over and over. You have to be tolerant. And you have to be flexible, adaptable.

Things change so quickly up there, and if you can't accept that sort of unpredictability, you're not going to make it.

UGOLYOK: I would say, get as fit as you can, physically and psychologically, so you're less likely to fall into a depression. You can't think that a trip into space is going to solve your personal problems. Once you're up there, those problems will not go away. They will come at you worse than ever before.

6. Blue Water Sailor

It was only in 1968 that the biomedical engineers shifted their attention from dogs and began to consider sending less conventional animals like me into space. They decided to take a chance and send a spaceship into orbit around the moon and back, and see what impact this lunar fly-by trip might have on the living creatures inside; a Noah's rocket-ark of biological specimens, including – finally – a little Russian tortoise. For once I could trump the dogs in the lab because, unlike them, I could survive on very little food, and Dr Yazdovsky was hoping I might even hibernate through the whole thing. I was to be one of the first animals of any kind to circumnavigate the moon. There was no way I was going to hibernate.

On 15 September 1968 our moonship, *Zond 5*, was launched. On board in the cabin, other than me in my terrarium, were some mealworms and wine flies, two spiders, lots of seeds, some plants, and bacteria in sealed Petri dishes. I had a good spot in the cabin, beside the clear porthole. I'd been washed with iodine and sprinkled with antiseptic powder where the electrodes were attached to my body. I felt good.

As the rocket full of explosives beneath our capsule propelled us up and out, I thought of Elizabeth Cady Stanton's words, the ones Alexandra had read aloud to me so many years before, and felt grateful to have my own thoughts to keep me company in this, my final lesson in solitude in my terrarium with a view of space. As we accelerated, as my vision dimmed and I could feel I was about to black out, I felt secure knowing I had been preparing for this my whole life, that I wanted nobody's company but my own.

When I regained consciousness, this sense of security had been replaced with the agony of banishment. I was being punished, exiled from earth like the original scapegoat in the Old Testament, a goat upon whose back all the sins of Israel were placed, and who was driven out into the wilderness for the demon Azazel. My shell felt as if it were made of metal, unbelievably heavy against my back. I was carrying the weight of all human sin, just as Oleg had said. What demon would be waiting for me behind the moon?

Once the main engine had been cut off, which I knew meant we had nearly reached orbital speed and would not fall back to earth, this paranoia dissolved. Microgravity felt wonderful. I hallucinated some music, an appropriate soundtrack for my out-of-body, out-of-earth experience: strange static chords, similar to the sounds received from the first radio contact with Venus. I did a small vomit, and felt better. I sensed in my weightlessness my blood pooling not in my feet but in my head and along the top of my shell, which felt weird but not unpleasant, like I was thick in all the wrong places. A thought occurred to me: Why do humans choose to see so many animals in the arrangement of the stars? Who joined the first dots?

Thoughts ceased for a while. When they returned, along with a headache, I wondered for a long time – minutes? hours? days? – if

I had gone blind, and it was with relief that I saw the light flashes I'd heard the dogs describing, which meant we were passing through the radiation belts. Things got lyrical. Through the porthole, on the way to the moon, I saw the earth. It was just as the dogs had described, a glassy illuminated marble. And yes, I did check, just once: there are no tortoises holding it up.

I watched one of the spiders squeeze its unbelievable way through the tiniest seam in the curved wall of our capsule, out into space. We are the new blue water sailors, just like the humans in the earliest days of sailing, the ones who were prepared to set off across the open ocean with no compass to guide them. The ones willing to sail out of sight of land, the ones who stirred up the world's organisms, taking them where they hadn't been and shouldn't have gone. One day, in the very far off future, when humans arrive on Titan, they will find pairs of dogs and monkeys waiting for them there, pairs of spiders and rats, and one very old Russian tortoise. It seems to be the curse of all earth's creatures, that we cannot help but spread ourselves around, always making a mess, carrying life with us, leaving it behind.

I decided space smells like ice – for I could smell it outside the capsule's walls – more sensation than scent. The spider was gone, escaped into the universe, already caught up in a stream of celestial plankton on the way to Titan. I thought of Darwin and the tiny exotic spider, no bigger than a poppy seed, that he'd noticed hitching a ride back to Britain on the rigging of the *Beagle*; how he'd thought it innocent, been blind to its hunger to rule a new world: 'The little aeronaut as soon as it arrived on board was very active, running about, sometimes letting itself fall, and then reascending the same thread; sometimes employing itself in making a small and very irregular mesh in the corners between the ropes.' Little aeronaut indeed.

I watched as the second spider, the one that had stayed behind in our capsule, began to spin a floating web in microgravity. This is when the solitude of certain death came upon me. I didn't know how to die, how one dies. In her depression before her suicide, Virginia had recited de Montaigne's words to herself: 'If you do not know how to die, never trouble yourself; nature will in a moment fully and sufficiently instruct you; she will exactly do that business for you, take no care for it.' I had spent my life in the company of writers who'd found their way to a perfect solitude: a hermit, a suicide, a vagabond, a lone avant-gardee; writers who had recognised in me a matching contradictory desire never to be let go of, always to be let alone. After the first blast of creation, we were all left homeless, every creature on earth.

The spider's threads grew thick. I thought of the legend of Charles Lindbergh's solo flight across the Atlantic in 1927, that in fact he'd had company in the cockpit in the form of a common fly. Afterwards he'd said it had given him solace knowing something else was alive in his cold little cabin, for all those solitary hours flying across the night ocean.

Around the moon we went, the spider and I.

I,
THE ELEPHANT,
WROTE THIS

Soul of Elephant

Died 1987, Mozambique

...why, some even say that man himself was made out of what was left over after the elephant had been created...

José Saramago, THE ELEPHANT'S JOURNEY

My twin sister and I, like all young elephants in our herd, were raised on a feast of stories about our ancestors, whose souls glowed at us from constellations in the sky. On certain summer evenings, the elders would point out identifying features among the stars: the tip of a trunk, or the triangular ends of an ear spread out in preparation for a charge – the same shape as the continent of Africa. They would tell us the story of one of these hallowed forebears looking down on us. My sister and I liked to re-enact what we had heard, living out an ancestor's great moments on earth and imagining what it might feel like to be transmuted into a soul that sparkles forever, wheeling about on an invisible axis.

It was clear to us from early on that only the ancestors who had died a noteworthy death made it into the stars. This fostered in us both a secret longing for a death deserving of a small legend that could be told and retold as the years and generations and eons passed. We decided that a dramatic individual death would be best, such as our ancient ancestor who was killed by a dragon wanting to drink her blood. But mass historical death would be grand – to die along with hundreds of thousands of beasts of burden sacrificed to Yahweh at Solomon's Temple, to be one of the five thousand animals ordered slaughtered by Roman Emperor Titus at the opening of the Colosseum, to be among the fifteen thousand killed in a single day's hunt by the Moghul Emperor of India! These outsized deaths seemed to guarantee eternal life in the stars.

Once my sister and I were a bit older, no longer babies coddled by the maternal force of the herd but still young enough to get away with certain mischief, I decided to ask one of my aunts why it was that all the ancestors whose stories were told and retold, whose distinguishing features we joined the star-dots up above to see, had lived in lands so far away from our native Mozambique. I knew she had a taste for marula bark because of the pleasant intoxicating effect of ingesting the beetle pupae embedded in the wood, and I waited until she was swaying slightly before I approached her.

'We don't make distinctions between our geographical lineages,' she said. 'We believe all elephants share a common ancestor, which makes us all kin, no matter where we live.'

'But so many of the ancestors in the skies are Indian elephants, or forest elephants from North Africa. What about the African savanna elephants, where are the stories about us?'

'Oh, but darling, there *are* stories about us, plenty of them. Most of the souls in the sky lived out their lives right here, in these lands.' Then she caught herself. 'How old are you and your sister now?'

'We're twelve,' I lied. We were only eleven.

She hiccuped. 'On second thought, I suppose there are fewer stories about us, because those Indian and North African ancestors of ours had more interesting lives,' she said. 'Being closer to Europe and all.'

I gave up on that line of questioning. 'But why did they all live so long ago?'

'It takes time for their souls to appear up in the sky,' she said.

I sensed my question had caused her some discomfort. 'How long?' I pushed.

'Well,' she said cautiously, 'which ancestor's story have you heard that is closest to our own time?'

'Castor and Pollux, the sibling zoo elephants,' I said. 'The ones who died in the Jardin des Plantes during the siege of Paris.'

'Well, there you go,' she said. 'That was – when was it? – around the year 1870? 1880? A hundred years ago. So perhaps that is how long it takes.' She wandered off to strip another marula tree of bark, and returned later in the day, singing loudly and walking in unsteady zigzags across the plain, to join the herd at our waterhole.

Once the sun had set, one of our baby cousins asked the elders to tell the story of our ancestor Suleiman, a story my sister and I had listened to many times with pleasure. But that night I didn't want to hear about faraway elephants.

'Suleiman was born in the royal stables of the King of Ceylon in the year 1540,' one of our great-aunts began. 'As a young boy, he was sent to Lisbon as part of a diplomatic outreach to King John III and Catherine of Portugal. Though he delighted them, they decided to gift him to their grandson Don Carlos. Suleiman travelled on foot to Spain, but Don Carlos found it too complicated to care for him. He was given to the Habsburg Archduke Maximilian II, who put him on a ship with his wife and children to Genoa. From there Suleiman travelled on foot again, all the way to Vienna, where a special celebration was held to welcome him to the city.

'In Vienna, Suleiman was given the honour of being the first animal housed in the menagerie within Maximilian II's newly built palace, the most beautiful Renaissance palace outside Italy. Here Maximilian tried to ensure his new pet's happiness. He gave orders that the elephant be fed the best exotic fruit from his orchards, and only the fruits Suleiman did not like were served at dinners in the imperial court. In the winter, Suleiman was given a gallon of red wine to drink every day, to warm his blood. On the stone blocks of the entrance to his spacious enclosure, Maximilian ordered one of the court's scholars to inscribe the words of the Roman historian, Pliny the Elder: *The elephant is the largest land animal, and also the nearest to man in intelligence. It understands the language of its country, obeys orders, remembers duties it has learned, likes affection and honours – more, it has virtues rare in man – honesty, wisdom, justice, and respect for the stars and reverence for the sun and the moon.*

'A giraffe was purchased to keep Suleiman company in the empty menagerie, but they did not take to each other, and the giraffe was eventually allowed to roam free in the palace gardens, where she developed a trick the noblewomen loved, of sticking her head through their first-floor windows for treats. Gradually, Maximilian expanded his menagerie as he expanded his empire, acquiring panthers and peacocks, lynxes and leopards, bears and buzzards. But he never managed to find another elephant to join Suleiman; some whispered it was because he didn't want Suleiman to bond too closely with one of his own kind.

'One day, when Maximilian brought his most pious priests to visit Suleiman, they found he had written something on the sandy floor of his enclosure: *I, the elephant, wrote this*. The priests were horrified. They insisted the elephant be killed on the spot, that his writing was proof of demonic forces at work. Maximilian refused, but he understood the risks enough to wipe out Suleiman's words with the sole of his own slipper. The priests took it upon themselves to have Suleiman secretly poisoned over the course of the next winter, adding arsenic to his daily wine.

'It took four months for Suleiman to die, and when he did, Maximilian was inconsolable. He told his servants to rub snuff in the eyes of all the other menagerie animals so that they would appear to be crying, in mourning as profound as his own. He decided that Suleiman's body should be divided up and distributed throughout the Holy Roman Empire so that his domain would never forget him.

'To the Mayor of Vienna, Maximilian gave Suleiman's right front foot and part of his shoulderblade – if you look up at the stars, see, there; can you see the shoulderblade and foot together? And next to them, if you join up that cluster of stars, you can see the chair that was made of Suleiman's bones, that to this day is in the abbey at Kremsmünster. His soul glows at us from these remnants. But most important is his stuffed skin – you have to draw an imaginary line from that trunk star to that tail star to see it – which was housed in royal collections and then in the Bavarian National

Museum for a long time, until the humans had their second great war of this century and it disappeared from the collection, never to be seen again.'

I waited for my great-aunt to sigh with contentment at the end of her telling, and for the herd around us to shift and settle. 'Is it because we don't have a museum?' I said. 'Is that why we don't tell the stories of our ancestors who lived here in Mozambique?'

'There is a museum, in Maputo,' said one of my cousins who had just come of age and was soon to leave the herd, before he was hushed by the elders and we were told by our mother, in no uncertain terms, to go to sleep.

Our oldest female cousin, who mostly ignored my sister and me though we followed her around devoutly, decided one day during a mini-rebellion against her mother's control that she would tell us the recent secret history of the herd in our own birthplace.

'There was a human war in our country that ended a few years after you two were born,' she whispered to us behind a scrub of thorn trees. 'Between the Portuguese and the local people, who wanted this country to be independent. You were too young to remember.'

'Were there any historically worthy deaths of our ancestors in this war?' my sister asked excitedly.

Our cousin looked over her shoulder before answering. 'Many of our clan were de-tusked and left to bleed out by the Portuguese as they fled the country,' she said.

'Right here? In Gorongosa National Park?' I said.

'Yes,' she said. 'Now you keep your little mouths shut. I'm not supposed to tell you these things. You'll find them all out when you're old enough.'

'When?' my sister said. 'When will we be old enough? We turn thirteen this year.'

She looked surprised we didn't already know. 'It is almost time for you to be initiated,' she said, her eyes softening.

'But nobody will tell us when that is.'

She pulled a strip of bark off an acacia trunk, exposing its pink underside, and gave a low rumble of frustration. 'You two have always had special treatment because you're twins. We didn't think you would survive at first. Your mother didn't have enough milk for you both, so one of the aunties shared her milk. The herd has cared for you and protected you from harm. When you are strong enough, you will learn what you want to know.'

Our cousin was right in saying the time would pass quickly, that we should not wish it away. Soon after my sister and I turned thirteen we experienced our first full night of wakefulness. Instead of falling asleep lying on the ground like the young elephants, she and I found we could not sleep. We kept company with the adult members of the herd, standing awake and protective above the sleeping children. Just before sunrise, we coiled up our trunks on our upturned tusks and dozed on our feet until the sun made the air bright. Only our great-grandmother, the matriarch of our herd, did not doze at all.

In the morning our mother told us we were ready to be initiated. 'This wakefulness is the first sign that you are ready to be mothers and leaders yourselves,' she said.

The herd waited for the full moon to arrive, and from the night it rose fat and red above the bush until the night it had melted away by half, we were initiated into the secrets of the herd and the principles by which we should live as adults.

On the third night of our initiation, the matriarch told a story.

'Many years before you two were born, something terrible happened here. There was a piece of land nearby that the Portuguese thought might be suited to growing crops. They ordered a local hunt supervisor to kill two thousand elephants living on the land. He followed his orders, but he had a scientific bent to his mind. He decided to cut out and collect every unborn baby he found in the wombs of the dead.

'His ambition grew. He could not stop until he had the world's only complete collection of elephant foetuses, one for every month of the twenty-two months of our gestation. When he had collected all twenty-two in ascending size, he had them preserved in formaldehyde and donated them to the curator of the Lourenço Marques Natural History Museum – this was before our capital was renamed Maputo – who still displays the jars.'

She looked at the sky. With her trunk she pointed to a knot of stars close together on the horizon and waited for my sister and I to count them. There were twenty-two.

'You have asked for the stories of your immediate ancestors,' she said. 'Their souls are inscribed up there too. But their stories are more difficult for us to tell our young. We have to start you on the tales of elephants from long ago and far away.'

She must have seen the excitement in our eyes at discovering a new layer of constellations in the sky dedicated to our own African ancestors. 'Death is not something to worship now that you are adults,' the matriarch warned. 'It is the province only of the very young to want things to work out badly. The souls in the sky live only as long as we remember their stories. Beyond that there is nothing, not for them nor for us.'

Though I had been told by the elders of the power it would give me over males, the effects of my first oestrus took me completely by surprise. Adolescent bulls from all corners of Gorongosa began to hang around our herd and wider bond group, gazing at me with open desire and shoving one another away to get a closer sniff of my urine. The attention was intoxicating. But the elders counselled me to ignore these too eager boy-men and wait for an older bull in musth to begin to court me. And soon one did, a bull in his thirties with secretions from his temporal glands streaming down his cheeks. I let him shadow me for a while, glancing over my shoulder at him and enjoying the sound of his calls while he followed. It was the only time in my life that I forgot the presence of my sister and all my family: my world had shrunk to the two of us in consort.

I knew immediately a new life had begun inside me and sang the deep, arched notes I had been taught during my initiation to summon my herd around me to celebrate. They trumpeted and flapped their ears, smelled the spilled semen on the ground, and rubbed their flanks against my stomach, rumbling with joy. My sister stayed by my side all the rest of that day and night, rejoicing. Her own oestrus began soon after. We carried our babies at the same time, through two of the longest, driest summers the herd could remember.

My difficult labour lasted for two days, assisted by my mother and aunts. Finally my daughter was born in her foetal sac, and within half an hour of her birth she stood up, fell over, and was gently nudged up again by my mother. She found her way to my teats and began to suckle. For hours I could not stop rumbling with pleasure and love, soothing her, reassuring her, sharing my wonderful news with our bond group and wider clan throughout the bush. I helped my sister birth her son in the spring days that followed. We laughed together as we watched our babies discover their trunks and try to figure out what to do with them. They would swing them around and back and forth, sucking on them, tripping over them, all the while bewildered as to what these strange things were useful for. At night we stood awake above our sleeping infants, keeping guard beside all the adult women in the herd.

Their new lives cauterised our old longing for a glorious death. My sister and I began to wish for beauty and goodness in life, and tried not to think of death at all. Immune to the old charms, we hardly listened at dusk when the elders told the herd's babies and children stories of long-dead foreign ancestors under the flowering cashew trees. When my baby girl looked up to piece together the outlines of Castor and Pollux in the sky, I felt nothing but quiet elation at having her skin against my own.

One day at the beginning of the second dry summer after their birth, I discovered my daughter and nephew painting mud in diamond patterns on each other's foreheads at the edge of the dwindling Lake Urema, arranging coral tree twigs into headdresses and pretending they were made of velvet brocade and gold thread.

I demanded to know what they were doing. My daughter told me they were pretending to be Castor and Pollux adorned in finery, giving imaginary Parisian children a ride around the zoo in the Jardin des Plantes. They couldn't understand my anger, which had its origins in fear, and they ran away and hid from me in the acacia grove. My sister said I had reacted badly by trying to stop their play-acting, that it would only encourage them as it had encouraged us at their age.

She took a different approach and told them everything they wanted to know about Paris and the siege, how the Prussians had encircled the city to starve the Parisians into surrender. She told them that the hungry Parisians had eaten their way through tens of thousands of the city's horses, until there was not a single horse to be found. Next they started in on the rats, but even the city's best chefs had not been able to make rat taste good, though they tried hard to entice the wealthy in the expensive dining clubs with cured rat sausage. Once every cat and dog in the city had been eaten, the chefs began to look around for other meat sources for their rich patrons. Rationing was never considered – the rich must eat meat regardless, and the poor were told they should survive on mustard and wine, of which the city had plenty stored.

I gave my sister a warning look.

'That's enough for today,' she said. 'Time to nap.'

The next morning, my daughter and her cousin talked a baby zebra into pretending to be a horse, and a bush rat into being a city rat, and they chased them as if they were human and hungry. It was normal for our young to test their powers by asserting play-dominance over other creatures in the bush, shooing them along with wide ears, trying to trumpet. The other women in our herd looked on with amusement. But I asked my sister to stop telling the tales, and she agreed for a while to let me distract our children with soft little stories about how the lion got its mane, and how the

Milky Way was created from ashes thrown up into the sky by one of our ancestors, to lead his lost lover home.

It was at this time that strange foreign humans began to occupy the rundown National Park tourist camps in our territory, abandoned since the Portuguese had left. For many years we'd had Gorongosa mostly to ourselves, disturbed only by locals from the villages just outside the park's reinforced fences who sometimes took shortcuts through the park, if they felt brave enough to come face to face with lions or buffalo. Some of our herd recognised the foreign men's collective scent from past travels over the Mozambique border into the enormous Kruger National Park on the South African side, before the electric fences separating us from our relatives were built. We watched from a safe distance as these men set up a shooting range. Soon they were bringing local men to the camp and teaching them to shoot at targets.

The elders decided we should be cautious and move further away, towards the eastern edge of Gorongosa. We moved at night while the men were sleeping. As a child, I had always loved walking along the eastern boundary because of the smell of the orange groves the villagers tended on the other side. The citrus scent was so overwhelming that the elders in our herd would collect near the weakest parts of the enclosure, knowing we youngsters would be unable to resist trying to get to the fruit. Oranges have always been our great weakness. But that night there was no heady citrus scent, only smoke from fires on the other side of the fence.

The next night we moved on again, towards the Muaredzi River. It was hardly flowing. Several monsoon seasons had given us very little rain and we had suffered through the resulting dry summers, but Lake Urema still had just enough water for us not to become anxious. Now we were unsure whether to return to Lake Urema and risk being close to the strange humans, or to stay and hope that by some miracle the Muaredzi's waters might begin to swell. Our matriarch decided we should stay and wait.

After many weeks of waiting, another herd within our bond group arrived, on their way to see if the Mussicadzi River further afield might be flowing more swiftly. We had known for a while that they were coming, having listened closely to the infrasonic sound waves they transmitted. We greeted one another joyously with chirps and barks and constant rumbling, and they spent several nights with us, telling us stories about what they had seen on their journey from the south. They said the foreign humans had many local recruits now, often from the surrounding villages; they burned the homes to the ground and forced the men to fight. Some of them were very young, closer to being children. Other humans had tried to attack the men's compound within Gorongosa from the air. The travelling herd had seen a pilot crash his helicopter and stagger out wearing a fur-lined aviator cap with an emblem on it that looked like the tools humans use to farm. A Russian, one of the elders said.

The other herd promised to return as quickly as they could, and left to follow their matriarch towards the Mussicadzi. When they finally came back to us, they said that river too was almost dried up. They said a different group of men had moved into the Lion House on the old floodplain near the river – a concrete building, open to the elements, that had been occupied by the same pride of lions and their descendants since the Portuguese abandoned their tourist camps. Now the lions had all disappeared or been killed. We worried about them, dying so secretly. Even the floodplain was dry.

The other herd had fewer babies to look after, and our matriarch and theirs decided it would be best for our herd to stay beside the Muaredzi for its meagre water, while they moved on and tried to find another supply. We held a formal farewell ceremony before they left, making a ring with our bodies close together, breathing in the smell of our kin.

All through the summer we watched the Muaredzi die a slow death, gradually reduced to a trickle. The adults drank less and less so that our young could have their fill. There was very little to eat – the savanna grasses were too dry, and most of the trees and shrubs we like to pull branches and leaves from had lost their sweetness and were dying too. We dug with our tusks for roots and tubers, for their stored moisture. At night we took extra care to keep our little ones surrounded, for the hyenas were becoming bold in their own hunger and thirst.

One hot afternoon, my sister distracted her son and my daughter from our troubles by caving in to their requests for more stories about Castor and Pollux.

'A zoo,' she said to them, 'is a very dangerous place for an animal in wartime, for it can mean the difference between life and death for the human inhabitants of a city. But it was not the poor who ate the zoo animals in Paris.'

Our children listened closely. She told them that the rich Parisians had started first on those zoo animals they could in good conscience eat, the ones that were not so far from the herbivores usually adorning their porcelain plates: two zebras, the yaks, five camels, a herd of antelope. Then they ate the flamingos and the single adored kangaroo. Next they shot and ate the lions and tigers. The zookeeper, desperate to save his beloved hippopotamus, said he would only sell it for food if somebody paid eighty thousand francs (the story was he'd been told a tale at his mother's knee about a hippopotamus). Not even the rich could justify such an expense when there were other zoo animals still to be eaten. They ate their way through the wolf pack, drizzled with deer sauce. Then they ate the passenger pigeons that had so faithfully been transporting secret messages from the French command in Tours.

I heard our children arguing afterwards.

'*I'm* Castor!' my daughter insisted. She was twirling her tail, trying to keep away the flies that kept landing in a black pall across her back.

'No, you're not,' her cousin said. 'You're Pollux.' And he stuck his little trunk in the air and paraded a bit, waiting for her to retaliate.

For once I was glad they had escaped to their make-believe Paris, relieved they still had the energy to pretend.

The next day I took over the telling from my sister. I told them that when it came to the monkeys the Parisians paused. They tried for a while to ignore their hunger. Some wrote editorials to be published in the gazettes, which were distributed around France by hot-air balloon (now that the passenger pigeons were all eaten up) to outwit the circling Prussians, declaring that sometimes it might be better to starve than to eat the meat of a creature that reminded them in some uncomfortable way of themselves, though they could not yet put their finger on exactly *what* or *why* that was. They did not credit us elephants with the same exceptional qualities, and so they turned away from the monkeys towards Castor and Pollux, who year after year had patiently borne the weight of the children of Paris on their backs. The chef of a fine-dining establishment on the boulevard Haussmann stepped forward and offered twenty thousand francs for the two elephants. The zookeeper accepted: his family was starving too. He shot Castor and Pollux with steel-tipped bullets in the middle of winter, while they were dressed in their finest headgear.

Our children had always known this was how Castor and Pollux died. But they were slightly older now, more curious about certain details.

'What do we taste like to humans?' my daughter wanted to know. She was still suckling, but had started to experiment with new tastes by trying bits of various bulbs from my mouth as I chewed, learning from me which were safe to eat.

I told her that the diners had complained that the trunk was too tough and the flank steak too oily, the consommé bland and the elephant-blood pudding bitter. One month after they ate Castor and Pollux, the French surrendered. The Prussians held a demure victory parade then sent food by train into the city. The sympathetic English sent over boatloads of pork pies and currant jam. The siege was over, the zoo animals gone.

In the night, my daughter woke and nudged my leg with her forehead. She looked up at me with serious eyes. 'I don't want you to die,' she said.

I stroked her small body with my trunk until her breathing

slowed again, not sure what to say. 'Are you still awake, sweetheart?' I whispered.

'Yes,' she said.

'Did Auntie tell you who the elephants Castor and Pollux were named after?'

'No,' she said, breathless with the pleasure of anticipating another story.

'There is a human myth from long ago,' I said. 'From a time when most humans worshipped many gods. They believed a mortal woman, Leda, had given birth to an unusual set of twins. The twins had different fathers, one a mortal named Tyndareus, and one an immortal god, Zeus. These twins were named Castor and Pollux. Castor was mortal, but Pollux was immortal.'

'Does that mean he couldn't die?'

'Yes, that he would live forever. Castor was killed in battle, and Pollux was distraught. He begged his father, Zeus, to make his twin immortal just as he was, so that they could be together for eternity. Finally Zeus agreed, and he transformed the twins into two stars in the constellation the humans call Gemini.'

'Is this the same constellation where we see the souls of the elephants Castor and Pollux?'

'Yes. We see the sibling elephant ancestors looking at each other in profile, foreheads pressed together, just one eye visible for each. And the humans see the immortal mythical twins, never separated.'

My daughter thought about this for a long time, looking up at the sky. Clouds began to efface the stars, but it would mean nothing. Each night the clouds grew purple and heavy, only to clear at daylight without a drop of rain. The first monsoon downfalls were long overdue.

'Are you the mortal twin?' she said finally. 'Or is Auntie?'

I smiled. Her logic was sound. 'When we die, our souls will appear together in the sky,' I said, not quite answering her question. 'We will always be watching over you.'

That night we heard the sounds of humans fighting one another with their technologies of fire, somewhere within the southern boundaries of the park.

When the Muaredzi had almost dried up, our matriarch decided we should move on again, towards a waterhole whose location was a closely guarded secret held only by the matriarch and the next most senior female within the herd. We travelled mostly at night, sometimes forced to keep going during the heat of the day if we could sense the humans were getting too close. They weren't searching for us – they were distracted by their desire to destroy one another – but we knew that our glowing tusks would be too tempting for men with guns to ignore.

We passed a bachelor herd from another clan, who refused to cede their precedence over the remaining edible grasses and barks, and showed scant interest in the eligible females within our family. It is one of the strictest rules for our species that new life should never be created in times of severe drought. Out of desperation our matriarch challenged them for access to the food, and we charged with her, but it led to nothing. The bachelors stood their ground.

But then something remarkable happened: my sister's son pushed his way to the front of our herd, through the legs and bodies guarding him, and began to nibble at a patch of grass that was somehow still green, right in front of a bull elephant. My sister and

I moved forward immediately to shield him. The bull looked down at him, then turned away and left us in peace. All the young children in our herd ate well that day. One by one, they became sleepy after feeding, sank down onto their knees, and fell over onto their sides to lie in the shade we created for them with our bodies.

When we reached the secret waterhole we drained what was left of it within a few days. Our matriarch determined the only thing to do was return to Lake Urema, despite the risk. On the journey some of the elders in our herd became listless, and we younger women had to nudge them and rumble to them constantly to keep them focused on moving. We began to pass the remains of animals killed and eaten by humans, left beside makeshift cooking fires. At first, only the usual: zebra, wildebeest, buffalo. But then we found a pack of wild dog carcasses and stopped to mourn for them. They are as closely bonded as we are, their packs woven together by mutual affection and trust. We spent time breaking branches to cover their bodies out of respect.

We stayed far from the old dirt roads of the park, except for one crossing we could not avoid, and found it destroyed. The longer route to Lake Urema took us through unfamiliar territory, tinder-dry like the rest of the park, and it was on this path that we discovered the dead body of the matriarch of the bond group that had left us at the Muaredzi, the same kind leader who had let us stay to drink the last of the water. Her herd must have been in terrible danger to have left her lifeless body uncovered.

My daughter and nephew had never seen a dead elephant before and were terrified of her body. My sister and I had to coax them to join us in grieving for her, moving backwards towards her body and gently touching her with our hind legs, then moving away to circle and hover around her, then forwards to touch her again. Our matriarch led us in keening and throwing sand over the body, then covering her with branches to ease her passage into the earth.

'Will her soul be in the stars tonight?' my nephew asked his mother.

It was still years before he would be old enough to be initiated. My sister looked at me and I nodded.

'Not tonight,' she said. 'But soon, when you look up at the sky, you will find her soul there. She died for her family. It is the most heroic death of all.'

For two days we kept vigil with our herd, standing quietly beside the matriarch's covered body, my sister's flank against my own, ignoring our thirst.

We were a day's walk from Lake Urema when they surrounded us. A group of hungry villagers no longer willing to wait it out on the other side of the park boundary, prepared to confront their terror of lions to come hunting for food. Not soldiers, not poachers, but starving families, come on foot. Our herd immediately closed ranks to protect the babies, pushing them into the centre and forming a protective barrier around them with our bodies.

Our matriarch charged, but the villagers had expected this. My sister, who was exposed on the outside ring of the herd, was shot and fell. I felt the herd trying to move me away, to keep me bundled within their vortex, the babies bound even more tightly within it, but I could hear my twin calling for me. I went to her and nudged her to get up and keep walking, and when she couldn't I lay down beside her. I don't remember being shot, or feeling any pain. I know she and I were both focused on the herd as they moved away with our children hidden from sight between their bodies, willing them to disappear to safety.

As we were dying, our foreheads pressed together, one of the humans stepped forward and placed a single orange in the gap between our trunks. It was an act of kindness, I think, a way to thank us for our sacrificed flesh. I was already too far from the appetites of life to eat it, but the smell made me briefly happy – we were children again, two sisters playing beside the fence separating us from a fragrant orchard of oranges, longing to die gloriously and have our souls pointed out to the youngest in the herd on warm evenings: see, there are the stars which form their trunks, and there are the stars of their tails.

TELLING FAIRYTALES

Soul of Bear

Died 1992, Bosnia and Herzegovina

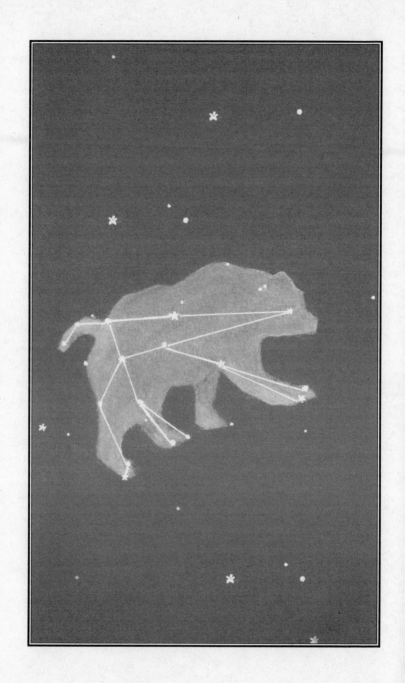

*What does it mean to be human? Perhaps only the animals
can know.*

Boria Sax, founder of Nature in
Legend and Story (NILAS)

'Witch, write this down,' said the black bear.

'Why should I?' said the witch, who had brought old bread to
the bear's enclosure. She split a loaf against her knee.

'You know very well I can't speak to humans without you,' the
bear said.

'I would counsel you, in this situation, to keep your dignified
silence and say not a word,' said the witch. She threw the bread, one
angular piece at a time, into the bear pit. 'Or you will be judged on
our terms.'

'So be it,' said the bear, ignoring the bread. He was sitting
in shallow water in a moat fed by the stream running through

the zoo's grounds.

'Eat, bear, before your friend wakes up,' the witch said.

'My friend,' the bear said sarcastically, looking at a sleeping brown bear in the cave at the centre of the enclosure. 'I'm waiting for her to die so I can eat her.' He chewed at the bread.

'Why wait?' asked the witch.

'People would stop risking their lives, dodging sniper bullets to bring me bread, if they thought I had no heart, eating her while she's still half alive,' the bear said.

Somewhere further down the slope of the hill in the city under siege, a shell landed, fired from the front line on the distant green and lethal valley ridge opposite.

'The stadium?' the witch guessed. 'The medical school?' She squinted a little until the answering smoke rose. 'Lion Cemetery. Another interrupted burial,' she said with something like satisfaction. But still she shrank a little, putting her body closer against the fence of the enclosure. It was late summer in Sarajevo, and thirst was driving more citizens of the city to risk being hit by enemy shells or snipers in their search for drinking water.

'I wish they would bring the bodies to me,' the black bear said. 'Instead of this bread.'

The witch didn't respond. She thought she'd seen movement across the deserted grounds of the zoo, near where the monkeys once lived, but it was just wind in the leaves of a lone oak tree. The zoo was trapped in a no man's land adjacent to the encircling front line of the Serb soldiers who had taken the city hostage. Not many trees had survived.

The bear lifted himself onto his hind legs and gazed through the fence with a carnivore's longing at the body of a Bosnian soldier who had been shot earlier that day bringing food from his own rations to the two bears, black and brown, the last surviving residents of the zoo. Nobody had yet been able to drag his body out of the clearing near the empty aviary, across the exposed ground back to the Bosnians' improvised military base. They were waiting for cover of night. 'How's black market business?' the bear asked the witch.

'Brisk,' the witch answered. 'Sugar and salt, bully beef, light bulbs, flour – the staples. I'm getting rich, in Marlboros at least.'

'Good for you,' said the bear.

In the cave, the stringy brown bear was stirring. She rolled onto her back and stretched. Her eyes were open but pale, blind. 'Hello?' she said. She sniffed the air.

The black bear rolled his eyes at the witch. 'Hey, fatso.' He crunched through the last loaf of bread.

The brown bear did not move from the entrance to the cave. She put one paw in her mouth and sucked on it. After a while she said, 'Hello, witch.'

The witch ignored her, lit a cigarette. 'There's something about smoking on a hot day that feels decadent,' she said to the black bear. 'Like eating ice cream in winter.'

The thin brown bear inhaled the smoke, and felt light-headed. It was the same brand of cigarette the head zookeeper and his wife had smoked. They'd liked to stroll along the manicured paths at dusk after the zoo was closed and the animals fed, smoking and talking about the things that are important to people in peacetime: the weather, back pain, bills needing settling, a funny cartoon in the newspaper.

'Once upon a time, a human baby, a prince, was turned into a bear,' the brown bear said.

'Here she goes again,' said the black bear to the witch.

'Let her waste her last breath on stories if she wishes,' the witch said. 'She'll taste better with a bit of fairytale still on her tongue.'

The blind brown bear licked the wound between her claws, and fixed her vacant gaze on the black bear. 'This baby was a Persian prince, destined for great things. But his mother had sought the help of a witch to make the king marry her, and her son was the price she agreed to pay. A year after his birth, just when she was beginning to think she'd beaten the spell, she woke one day to find a bear cub swaddled in her son's crib. Terrified that the king would discover her secret, she turned the little bear out of the palace, whispering to him as she set him down in a forgotten fold of the mountains that he should go as far away as he could, and never come home.

'Now, this little cub did not know it as he fell into a lonely, trembling sleep, but a young Pole named Karol was among a group of soldiers walking through those same mountains, a father who had survived great hardship in a war camp far away in Siberia. These were the early days of the Second World War, and men everywhere were on the move.

'Karol discovered the bear asleep, his paws twitching as he dreamed. While Karol stood watching, the cub gave a snore so loud he woke himself up, and Karol immediately fell in love with him. He had watched his own baby boy sleeping the night before his arrest in Poland, after the Russians invaded. Every day in the camp in Siberia, and every day since the Russians decided to let the Polish prisoners of war go freely to their deaths fighting the Germans instead, he had longed to hold his son's tiny body against his chest, to feel his rapid miniature heart beating against his own.

'That night, when the men made camp, the bear slept beside Karol, curled into an enamel washing-up bowl. The other men laughed at this, but not as much as you might expect, and soon they were competing for the bear cub's affections, coaxing him back down the tree trunks he liked to climb at perilous speed, holding his paws so that he could learn to walk like an unsteady toddler. But the cub returned each night to sleep in his enamel bowl beside Karol.

'There was never any question of whether the bear would come with them when they set off again, moving through the mountains towards British Palestine, where the men were to be regrouped and absorbed into the Polish army. No time to come to terms with anything that had happened or to mourn any loss; no time for anger about the cattle trains they'd been packed onto in Poland to carry them to Siberia; no time to rejoice at being free from the camp or to fear the death that freedom might hold within it – for there was a war to fight.

'When they arrived in Palestine, Karol's transition into his new regiment was eased by the bear, who was adopted as their mascot and enthroned on an upturned bucket to keep court outside the tent of the commander himself. There he sat like a regular little prince, unperturbed by the sandpaper winds that blew in across the desert, slowly drinking a beer in the worst of the day's heat. Often he could be found beneath the water truck taps, and anybody who passed could not resist dousing him, for his gaze was so direct, so beseeching. When Karol took his shower in the ablutions hut, the bear came with him, and there in the middle of the naked men he would stand lathering his little belly as naturally as could be.'

At this point in the brown bear's story, the black bear cleared his throat. 'We've got visitors,' he said.

It was dark in the zoo by now, darker than it had ever been before the siege started, for the city of Sarajevo no longer relied on electricity. It had become medieval, lightless, its citizens forced to fetch water from underground springs and to wash by candlelight. And the zoo was no longer a modern thoroughfare for the ogling masses. Now the few who dared visit brought sacred offerings of food. The two last remaining animals had become central to the city's very survival, to the idea of the city's survival.

The witch withdrew into the shadows. Two men were approaching the cage, a soldier and his much younger brother, a boy of no more than sixteen. They paused at the fence, their eyes adjusting to the deeper darkness within the pit, trying to see the bears.

'Where are they?' the younger one whispered.

'There,' his brother said. 'There are two, one black and one brown. You can see their eyes shining.' He threw the bunch of nettles they'd brought for the bears into the enclosure.

The brown bear moved out of the cave, allowing herself to be seen more clearly.

'Do you remember them?' the older brother whispered. 'From when we used to come here when you were little?'

'This one is blind,' his brother said. 'The brown bear is blind.'

'She was always blind. Don't you remember?'

The young brother stood and looked in turn at the black bear and the brown bear, and realised that he had never had his gaze returned by any animal at the zoo.

The older brother's thoughts turned to their parents, hoping they had taken his advice not to go outdoors together anymore, though their parents had never, in their twenty years of marriage, not taken their morning walk in the park to feed the birds by hand. The birds were mostly gone now, a rare sighting in Sarajevo that summer.

The witch waited a while after the brothers had left before slipping out of her hiding place. She lit another cigarette and brazenly smoked it, announcing to anybody who might be watching from a distance that she was there, alive, smoking.

'You know what I miss,' she said. 'Ripe strawberries. I could smell them from my apartment window when spring arrived, when the wind blew in from the east, from the fruit fields. But nobody could get to them because of the barricades around the city. Same with the new potatoes. Rotted in the soil.'

'One of the soldiers tossed me a snail a few days ago,' the black bear said derisively. 'A *snail*. Think of it. And he threw it to me with regret, as if he were throwing me a steak marbled with fat.'

'Snails are all the rage in the city,' the witch said. 'Pity there's no butter to eat them with. They don't taste right boiled and bare. That's all snails are, really, an excuse to eat butter.'

The brown bear took a startled, rattling breath. She was determined to keep telling her story about the human prince turned into a bear.

'By the time Karol's regiment was moved to Iraq – the Germans were nearby, threatening the oil fields – the bear was no longer a cub,' the brown bear said. 'With his simple animal presence he had elevated them all, every single soldier, above their slogging daily tasks. Those in charge saw beyond this sentimentality – they knew a good mascot could do wonders for productivity, keeping the men hard at work supporting the shifting lines in the Middle East.

'There, at their new base, to the men's great delight, were

women – and, even better, they were Polish women, members of the Women's Signal Corps, camped alongside them in an even drier desert than the one they'd just left in Palestine. The men and women were encouraged only to mix at mealtimes, and some parts of the camp were segregated, but the heat made everybody lax. One afternoon, as the men and women sat down together in the balmy mess tent to eat lunch, the bear appeared with ladies' underwear draped over his head and one very large-cupped beige brassiere caught in his claws. Not only had he stolen their under-wear in a stealthy raid on the clothesline in the women's camp, but he'd decided to take the pole too, and he marched up and down and around the mess area holding it up like a rifle, in perfect mimicry of a military drill.

'When those in charge decided he should be punished, the bear put his paws over his eyes and looked truly ashamed, and nobody – not a single man – would agree to take up the pole and administer the punishment. The bear was careful to look contrite for a couple more days, until Christmas arrived and all the women spoiled him with figs and dates, and a whole jar of honey to himself.

'Karol afterwards swore he hadn't taught the bear this trick of stealing underwear (though in truth he wished he had), but the women decided to take their revenge on the men anyway. Leaving the door to the men's storeroom open, where the precious supply of beer was kept, they encouraged the bear to help himself. He drank ten bottles and passed out. When he revived, the women snuck him into the men's wash hut, and by the time he was discovered having a lovely reviving splash, he'd used up two days' worth of their washing water. After that, a truce was struck.

'The night before the men's company was due to move on to

Egypt, almost every man in Karol's regiment crept into the women's camp to say goodbye to a new sweetheart. Karol sat in his tent with the bear, wanting more than anything to go and lie beside a woman called Irena, who at Christmas had given him a stack of handkerchiefs she'd embroidered with his initials, and who had a gorgeous streak of grey through her otherwise auburn hair. He thought about his wife and baby son, now no longer a baby, and when he found he could not quite recall his wife's face he began to cry. The bear, alarmed, nestled against his side and thought of his own human mother: her hair falling into his face as she leaned into the cot, the apricot smell of her as she nursed him.

'There was a sound outside the tent. Irena's face appeared through the opening. She crawled inside and sat on the other side of the bear, so that she and Karol were not touching, and began to tell a story.

'"Once upon a time," Irena said, "a handsome king decided to take a stroll through the gardens of his royal menagerie, admiring the ostriches' plumes glowing rose-grey at dusk, feeling the pleasant ache in his shoulders from the day's ring-hunt. He was feeding a plum to one of the zebras when the bear spoke to him.

'"*Would you like some honey?* the bear said to the king. She was sitting on her back legs and using her paws to eat a waxy chunk of honeycomb.

'"The king had never heard an animal speak before, but he welcomed mystery and was not afraid. He joined the bear in the secret terraced garden in which she lived. Together they ate the honeycomb and watched as the king's courtiers lit the slow-burning balls of lignite in the palace grounds below, ready for the evening's games. The bear began to sing a ballad of such beauty that the king fell instantly in love with her. As the dew formed on the grass, they embraced.

' "In the morning, when the king awoke in pain from sleeping on the ground, he did not at first remember what had happened. The bear was still asleep beside him, a warm, wild body, and he thought for a moment that he had fallen asleep on a hunt, beside his dying quarry. What unnatural magic had made him fall in love with a beast such as this? He looked at her sleeping body and was overcome with revulsion and shame. He fled her enclosure and ordered that she be exiled from his kingdom. For the rest of his days he lived with the twin agonies of heartbreak and disgust: he never stopped loving her, nor loathing himself.

' "In her exile to the cold islands of the west, the bear gave birth to a daughter, who like her mother was cursed: a human princess trapped inside a bear's body, with gifts of speech and song and poetry so refined that her mother knew the same fate would befall her daughter, and her daughter's daughter, and so on forevermore; men would fall in love with them and then destroy them, and themselves, trying to purge this unclean love from their souls. And so it was, and so it still is, and so it will always be."

'Irena had finished her story. She reached over and lifted Karol's hand, kissed it once.

' "I have a wife," he managed to say in apology, in explanation for his heartless inaction.

'She said softly, "And I have a husband."

'The bear was evicted from the tent then, quite unceremoniously. Feeling abandoned, he was seized with the urge to run away, and off he loped into the desert. But before he could get very far across the sand, the Dalmatian he detested, with whom he had to share the camp's affections, began to howl and bark from his post, giving the bear away. Karol fed him treats out of guilt. The bear fell asleep sucking on a date pit, dreaming of the human princess trapped like him in a bearskin, the only woman who might find it in her heart to love him back.'

In the concrete cave in the Sarajevo zoo, the brown bear had run out of strength. Her mouth was dry, her hips were hurting. She turned her face in the direction of the black bear, sniffing the air between them as if it were sweetly perfumed, intimate. Then she folded herself carefully into the corner of the cave and fell into a feverish sleep. When she woke, the soldier's body was no longer in the clearing, and she could sense from the more brittle morning air that summer was over.

Some weeks passed. The people who brought food to the bears, soldiers mostly, but every now and then a brave, impervious civilian, seemed confused by the season's change. The romance of autumn's tentative beginning had thrown them just as the frothing cherry blossoms had early in the siege. They caught themselves feeling a familiar nostalgia, the same longing they'd felt at the start of every autumn, at the end of every summer, and they felt betrayed. This peaceful smudging of the colours of the city, this lovely crisping of the air: had the planet not noticed? Why did the change of season still bring with it thoughts of reapplying oneself to pursuits – a return to work, to school, to routine, to betterment – when there could be no return to any of these?

Now, the sharper the autumn air, the deadlier, for it was fog or rain alone that could give the city respite from the snipers' relentless surveillance. Winter would be better, perpetual winter would be the right season for a siege. Twigs, trunks, stumps, whole root systems of trees were disappearing from the streets and parks of Sarajevo, to be sold midwinter to desperate families who had burned their way through furniture, floorboards, wooden snow-shoes that the winter before had carried them across the fresh powder of the ski resort at Pale.

The sirens gave off their timeless moans of measured panic; the Sarajevo Centre for Security broadcast its dispatches:

> The city is relatively calm. A few shells have hit the district of Marindvor, and two or three buildings have been destroyed. From the Lukavica barracks missiles have been fired at the Oslobođenje building, and anyone who has no urgent reason for being in that area is advised to stay away for at least an hour. We will let you know when the area is safe again. You are advised to avoid long lines in front of bakeries or district offices that distribute ration cards; the rocket launchers are aimed at targets where people congregate. Electricity and water services are still interrupted, but we are working on their restoration. Don't leave your homes unless it is absolutely necessary. You have heard the sirens sound a general alert. Otherwise, it is a nice sunny day . . .

On a foggy night, one of the quietest since the siege began, a group of important foreigners made the pilgrimage to feed the bears, escorted by Bosnian militiamen.

A man wearing a flak jacket and new beige boots dropped his piece of bread through the railings and said to the man in a puffy winter coat beside him, 'We've done it before. Airlifted dogs out of Beirut to animal shelters in Utah. Civil wars tend to be hardest on animals.'

The woman in the small group took exception to this. 'You mean, compared to your normal, garden-variety war, when everybody is real careful about not stepping on any bugs on their way to the slaughterfields?'

The puffy-coated man spoke quietly. 'But you must see what sort of position this would put us in. Smuggling two bears out of Sarajevo in a food-relief convoy – what does that say to the people left behind? Why bears, not babies? I mean, a busload of children trying to get out of the city was fired on, and we're spending time worrying about these wild animals? We can't allow it, I'm afraid.' He was the only one who had not brought stale bread in his pockets for the bears.

The black bear was making an elaborate show of leaving some of the bread for the brown bear, knowing how much humans favour displays of fairness in animals. The brown bear did not touch it, however, rousing herself just enough to please the humans, coming forward to reveal her pitiable body and her opaque eyes. Old habits.

'Oh, this one's blind,' the woman said. 'Poor dear darling, poor angel. Has she always been blind?'

One of the militamen answered, 'Yes. Since she came to the zoo as a baby.'

'Malnutrition, probably,' the woman mused. 'And the other bear,' she said, looking more closely at the black bear, who was pacing up and down in front of the moat, eyeballing her. 'Has he always been this . . . this restless?'

'He's a bear in a zoo, madam,' the soldier said flatly.

'I know, I know, I don't mean —' She stopped, embarrassed.

The man in the new boots turned to her. 'It happens sometimes, to animals in captivity. Zoochosis, it's called. They go a bit nuts, do strange things, pace obsessively, lick the walls, sway, pull their fur out, hit their heads against the bars. And that would have been even before the shelling started.' This man had A+ stencilled on one of his chest pockets: his blood type in case he was wounded and the city's dwindling blood stores hadn't dried up entirely, in case somebody paid attention.

'That's the thing,' the man in the puffy coat said. 'They're just going to end up in another zoo someplace else. Still crazy.'

'Do you know what Sarajevo – the name – means?' the woman said to nobody in particular. 'The Turks gave the city its name. It means *palace in the fields*. Isn't that beautiful? Palace in the fields.'

The militiamen snapped their heads around in unison, towards a sound in the darkness. From the farthest edge of the siege line, across the valley, a missile blurred its way through the fog. A warning that tonight's ceasefire was the briefest of reprieves, that if it weren't for the fog, the fireworks would have burst until daybreak.

'That one looked like it was shot from the Osmica,' a soldier said under his breath, and one or two of the other militiamen laughed.

'It used to be a popular nightclub on the mountain,' the puffy-jacketed man explained to the other foreigners. 'Now the Serbs have made it into a bunker.'

When they'd left, the black bear ate the rest of the bread, and the witch emerged, yawning. 'I've got a joke for you. What's the difference between a clever Bosnian and a dumb one?' she said to the black bear. 'The smart one calls the dumb one in Sarajevo every day. From abroad.'

The black bear stared hard at the witch as if he didn't get it.

The witch fidgeted. 'Go on, then,' she said to the brown bear. 'We've got nothing better to do. Tell us some more about that prince who was turned into a bear.' She winked at the black bear. 'And they think *you're* the crazy one.'

The brown bear looked hopeful. She sat back on her haunches, tried to get comfortable, though she could feel the bones of her pelvis pressing against the concrete floor of the cave.

'The prince – in his bearskin – had grown,' she said. 'When he stood on his hind legs he was twice as tall as Karol, a towering mass of brown fur topped with a black nose. He liked to play-wrestle with the other soldiers, tumbling around in the sand, amazingly tender with the men despite his claws and his yellow teeth.

'By now the regiment had moved on to a place called Qassassin. Soon they were to set sail for Italy, to the real war – for often it felt to Karol as if they were playing at war in the Middle East. They worked hard, yes, transporting military equipment to other units in the area, in Syria or back to Iraq, and on any journey Karol made in the supply trucks, the bear accompanied him, squeezed between two men in the front seat. But the atmosphere in the camp was often festive, and the tents resembled a schoolboys' dormitory: packs of cards scattered around, and dirty socks, and dirtier cartoons poking out beneath the mattresses. There were cute animals everywhere you looked – ferrets, piglets, puppies, foxes, owls, ducks; each regiment seemed to have adopted its own live mascot. Karol liked to think the bear was different, beyond a mascot, that the bear was really, truly *one of them*. When they sailed for Italy, he would not let the bear be left behind at the sea's edge like all the other half-witted animal mascots. Karol had a plan.

'It was early in 1944 when the order came to embark. At the

quay in Alexandria, watching enormous cranes load trucks onto a liner converted into a troopship, Karol thought again of children playing at war: dwarfed by the crane, the trucks and tanks looked like Dinky toys, small enough to grasp in one fist. He looked at the bear beside him and tried not to panic. The time for petitioning was over – every favour had been called in, every application made – and now it was up to those in the British High Command to decide the bear's fate.

' "Corporal?" the liaison officer called from within the quay office.

'Karol answered automatically, "Sir?"

' "Not you," the man said. "I'm talking to the bear."

'When the MS *Batory* sailed later that day with a protective convoy and the Polish flag raised, Corporal Bear sat in a spacious cage on deck and chomped his way through his cigarette rations, doubled because of his size. The Persian prince in his bearskin was now officially a Polish soldier, granted a special travel warrant to stay with Karol's regiment for the duration of the war.

'When the ruins of the monastery above Cassino first became visible, this place where so many men on both sides had died – were dying – in agony, their souls too fresh to join the ancient ghosts of the Benedictine monks, Karol knew he should never have brought the bear with him. Yet he was guiltily glad of the bear's presence beside him on the steepest of the narrow mountain passes, as the truck followed the eerie, disembodied glow of a white towel hung about the shoulders of another soldier walking in front. This was the only way, as they moved through the chemical fog designed to keep their movements secret from the Germans, to have some idea of the curves of the road without headlights. The bear sat with his paws over his eyes most of the time, a gesture so ridiculously human that it made Karol smile in the trickiest moments of manoeuvring the truck, keeping him calm.

'The new traumas – camping below the monastery, watching its silhouette appear against the dawn sky, knowing that most of the Polish soldiers sent the night before to cross the Rapido River to reach the hill town had drowned – did not dull Karol's older ones: the last sight of his baby son, the cattle train, the icy alien gulag. It felt instead as if each one pulled at the same psychic tear in the fabric of himself, and might split that fabric in two. Only the bear kept Karol human, or better than human – kept him just whole enough to remain kind. *I am because you are*, he said to himself over and over, looking at the bear asleep beside him. *I am because you are.*

'One morning, after six days and nights of such violent shelling it had been impossible to sleep or think, they saw a lone Lancers Regiment pennant flying from the monastery's ramparts. Somebody had risked his life to attach it to the highest remaining wall, to let it be known that the battle was won.

'That same morning, to take his mind off his grief – a battle won on paper, but so many drowned, stabbed, exploded or sliced apart by bullets – Karol did a sketch of the bear carrying an artillery shell on his shoulder. He asked a friend to make a badge of this logo, and soon everybody in the company had it on their sleeve or hat or lapel. It was easy to get approval for it after the enormous losses the Poles had suffered, losses they were told had not been in vain, for the Cassino victory led to others. Rome fell, and Ancona, and finally Bologna. By the start of the following summer, the Germans had surrendered.

'Within days of the end of the war, Karol entered into one of the happiest times in his life, a voluptuously, almost indecently carefree time of limbo, with no decisions to make or responsibilities to take on because his fate was in the hands of the Allies. And all the while he knew that at the end of this sumptuous period of rest he would be reunited with his wife and son.

'He and the bear were granted a furlough on the Adriatic coast, billeted on a small farm run by a childless elderly couple. Their hosts did not seem to be grieving any specific losses, and the lack of a common language meant there could be no complicated conversations about guilt and blame. Mostly they co-existed in luxurious silence.

'Karol and the bear spent most days on the beach, along with most of their regiment, who had been billeted in the same area. Karol lay on his back and dug his feet under the sand, and imagined the same scene repeatedly: returning home with the bear by his side, ambling along the main road into his village, and seeing the look of joyful disbelief on his little boy's face.

'His reveries were interrupted at least once a morning by female screams, and every time, his blood moved more quickly from shock; for so long he had heard only male noises of distress. Then the screams would be replaced by laughter and strings of Italian curses, for the bear had snuck again into the sea and surfaced in the middle of a group of female bathers. For this trick the other soldiers rewarded the bear handsomely with cigarettes, for of course the women had to be apologised to and placated, and then names and smiles were exchanged and halting conversations in Italian begun.

'But months passed and Karol's euphoria began to fade as he watched his homeland being toyed with like a puzzle piece. Torrid deals were made with Stalin. The men were told they would be sent to Scotland to be demobbed instead of going home. They heard terrible stories about soldiers who had been prisoners of war, the few who were brave or sentimental enough to return to Soviet-occupied Poland, being put back on cattle trains to new death camps, or to familiar Siberian ones, or sent to the fatal gold mines of the Arctic Circle. They were told to be cautious, to bide their time.

'At Winfield Camp for displaced persons in the Scottish Borders, it was almost impossible to get information from the Soviet-occupied Polish territories – letters were being censored both ways. But Karol kept trying, writing to his wife and relatives, until finally somebody took pity on him and risked writing in a coded way the truth Karol already knew: that his wife and child were no longer alive.

'After this, Karol stopped caring about what might happen to the bear. The other Poles at Winfield watched the bear swim in the frigid edges of the nearby river and told stories about him to anybody who would listen. They sent him on missions to Karol, to do some funny new trick that might restore their connection, but Karol looked at the bear uncomprehendingly.

'When he was informed that the bear would be going to live in Edinburgh Zoo, Karol's first feeling was envy: if only he could live in an enclosure too, be fed and watered, not ever have anything asked of him again. He was invited to accompany the bear to Edinburgh, to walk him into his new enclosure and remove the chain from around his neck. All this he did, feeling nothing. He built a little pyramid of cigarettes on the ground, and opened a bottle of beer for the bear.

'When it was time to leave, he turned to the bear and put his hands automatically in the creature's paws. They looked at each other. The bear leaned forward and gave Karol's cheek a long, mournful lick. He knew he would never see Karol again, though they would live out their lives in the same city. Karol later heard that the bear was in love with a female bear brought to join him in his enclosure. He courted her with such ardour that the whole of Edinburgh was swept up in their romance. Sometimes, on better days, Karol would think of the story Irena had told him, of a human princess trapped in a bear's body, searching for love. And he would tell himself that tomorrow, *tomorrow*, he would find the courage to return: to the bear, to his homeland, to himself.'

The blind brown bear had finished her story. She lumbered down to the dirty water in the moat and began to scrub herself. A ritual cleansing, a preparatory rite. When her fur was soaked through, she returned to the concrete cave and lay down against the wall, shivering and pure.

The witch lit a cigarette stuffed with tea leaves and ignored for a moment the scornful eyes of the black bear regarding her. 'So I made some bad business decisions,' the witch said. She fiddled with the dial of a radio she'd brought with her, finding only static.

Below them in the city basin, the chocolate factory was burning. The smoke smelled of caramel. Voices surfaced out of the radio's static, clinging to the pirated frequency, not letting go.

'What is my wife saying? I can't hear. Say it again please?'

'She said that she is fine, that the children are fine.'

'Pardon?'

'That the children have grown.'

'What is she saying now?'

'That she misses you.'

'What?'

'She says she misses you.'

'I can't hear.'

'She says she loves you.'

'Excuse me?'

'That's okay, she says she's doing fine.'

'Please, I can't hear you!'

A day later, the brown bear died. The black bear ate her, limb by limb.

'What was it you really wanted to say?' the witch said to the black bear, pushing bread that rasped like stone through the fence railings. 'You asked me to write something down a while ago.'

'I can't remember,' said the bear, sucking contemplatively on the brown bear's thigh bone. 'It couldn't have been very important. These days I seem to exist only in the present. I can't remember anything from yesterday, or the day before that.'

'You do know what you've done, bear?' said the witch cautiously. 'Tell me you know.'

The black bear looked at her with contempt. 'What are you talking about, witch?'

The witch looked afraid. 'I thought you knew,' she said, preparing to leave. She gestured at the brown bear's clean bones. 'She was your wife.'

The black bear did not speak again. On an icy day at the end of October, he died with his paws wrapped around the brown bear's ribcage, holding it close against his body. In the nearby enclosures, the lay of the bones – once tigers, pumas, leopards, wolves, lions with beating hearts and wet tongues – told the same story: life mates eaten in madness, bones within bones, beloved consumed at last by their lovers.

A LETTER TO SYLVIA PLATH

Soul of Dolphin

Died 2003, Iraq

Dear Ms Plath

            I'd like to try to get the story of my death out of the way: no more of this terrible anticipation. This is the soldier in me speaking. I have the US Navy to thank for training me to do the deed, then deal with the deed, though it's in failing to deal that I died. Word games as primers, Ms Plath, you'd appreciate that.

The other animals who have told their stories here are not as burdened by previous and often foolhardy attempts at cross-species communication as I feel I am. We have a ridiculous history together, humans and dolphins, made more ridiculous each time a dolphin raises her head from the water and hams it up for the camera, or performs another inane trick for the sake of a tossed fish. Scientists have tried to transform us into serious objects of study, but even then there is something a bit off about what happens when they get down to work. Marine biologists start writing tacky utopian tracts about the possibilities of telepathic communication with us; animal behaviourists can't resist trying to get us to tap away at underwater keyboards to break codes. Science fiction writers generally use their poetic licence to imagine screwing us, which is unsurprising; we have long understood that we occupy a special place in the human erotic imagination.

So when I was first asked to tell my story, I thought, *Absolutely not*. But the brief became more interesting when it was suggested I think about a human writer who meant something to me, and let my thoughts of him or her infuse whatever I decided to say. I said I'd participate only if I could use the third person, to avoid becoming a parody of myself, the self-aware dolphin wielding 'I' like a toy ball propped between my fins. But as it turns out, 'I' is irresistible.

I began by rereading the work of your ex-husband, the British poet Ted Hughes, thinking I might be inspired by him. His famous animal poems were already familiar to me but I realised, as I read them again, that I had misunderstood them on first encounter. Back then, I had admiringly thought he was trying to understand the human by way of the animal, but now I can see that in fact he wanted to justify the animal in the human. I saw right through his mythologising of the poetic process, the animal as symbol of the poet getting in touch with his deepest, wildest, most predatory instincts. The poet as shaman, returning to primordial animal awareness. The poet saying, You have no idea how *alive* you can feel when you've been fishing all morning and fornicating all afternoon! Go forth, fish and fuck yourselves stupid, and you can thank me afterwards. We're animals, after all!

Hughes collected animal skins to put on the floors of the homes you and he lived in together, and I imagine he laid them out with great reverence, with not a hint of ironic kitsch. He justified hunting wild animals thus: 'Do you know Jung's description of therapy as a way of putting human beings back in contact with the primitive human animal?' It was all a licence to behave badly. I've got nothing against bad behaviour per se, but men – dolphin or human, and here again we are similar – do tend to weave a web of intricate justification around any wrongdoing, and it's this that drives me nuts. Women behave badly and then, because we don't have the ego necessary to sustain the same justificatory web, die of guilt.

I turned to the animal poems Hughes wrote for children, fables that he claimed would help them understand their unconscious thoughts and feelings. This is going to make us money, he told you, his young wife, as he churned one out every morning of your honeymoon in Benidorm before settling down to his real writing. Let's sell them to Disney! You didn't mind, you were worried about money. But the poems didn't make much, perhaps because most of them are wholly inappropriate for children, full of lines about carving knives, murderous relatives, stiff brandy, shark attacks, and one rather bizarre bent hypodermic. The only poem that got it right, 'Moon-Whales', which is both tender and off-key in the way children like, happened to be inspired by my own species (dolphins are toothed whales, but not many people think of us as such). For a while I thought I might write my contribution from the point of view of his mythical moon-whale, the most magnificent of all the creatures he imagines living on the moon.

But still it didn't seem right. I wondered, What is it I'm resisting here? I turned to your own work – your journals, your poetry – at first to counterbalance the relentless maleness of Hughes's writing voice. And you helped me understand what it was. That human women need no reminder that they're animals. So why do your men keep shouting it from the rooftops as if they've discovered how to transform base metals into gold? Imagine a male dolphin who has to keep having epiphanies to remember he's an animal! But we're *special*, your men declare, we're a special-case animal, and part of what makes us special is that we ask the very question, Am I human or animal?

So I ask them in turn, Can you use echolocation to know exactly what curves the ocean floor makes in every conceivable direction? Can you stun the creature you would like to eat using sound alone? Can you scan the bodies of your extended family and immediately tell who is pregnant, who is sick, who is injured, who ate what for lunch? The tingling many humans report feeling during an encounter with us isn't endorphins, it's because we've just scanned you to know you in all dimensions. We see through you, literally. Special case indeed. Perhaps you should be asking yourselves different questions. Why do you sometimes treat other people as humans and sometimes as animals? And why do you sometimes treat creatures as animals and sometimes as humans?

I floated all this with a friend I've made recently out here, the soul of Elizabeth Costello, an author and philosopher of sorts. She was unimpressed by my ranting. She feels attacking Ted Hughes for harnessing animals for his primitivist poetic purpose is not doing him justice, and that it would be thoroughly unoriginal to take him to task for it.

'It is an attitude that's easy to criticise, to mock,' she said. 'It is deeply masculine, masculinist. Its ramifications in politics are to be mistrusted. But when all is said and done, there remains something attractive about it at an ethical level.'

When I protested, she cut me short. 'Writers teach us more than they are aware of,' she said. She suggested I focus instead on what I want to say to you, Ms Plath. 'Why a letter?' she wanted to know.

I explained that Hughes thought of letter writing as good practice for conversation with the world. I agree with him about that, though clearly not about much else.

Then she pointed out that despite my determination to get it out of the way early, I've been avoiding the issue of my death, and rather well too. It's harder to get around to than I thought it would be. In part, I think, because when I decided to write this letter to you, it had less to do with the way we both died and more to do with the connection I felt to you as a fellow mother. I have one child; you had two. You might not know that the Greek root of our name, *delphis*, means womb – we are the womb fish – but I think you would have liked the term, even used it in one of your poems.

By far my favourite parts of your journals and poems are the insights you share into the quicksand, joyous minutes and hours and days and weeks and years of mothering, and how you did not think of this experience as something that encroached on your other identities, but as something which enriched them. You were not a frustrated housewife forced to stick your head in the oven and turn on the gas because your desire to write had been subsumed by the mundane, miraculous hourliness of being a mother. You describe your priorities so poignantly in one of your journals as *Books & Babies & Beef Stew*; and for a while, you had the promise of all three – writing in the mornings, caring for your babies in the afternoon, cooking rabbit stew in the evenings if your husband had shot one in the woods, reading at night. Virginia Woolf, as you noted in your journal, described in her own diary receiving a rejection letter from a publisher and dealing with it by frying up a big panful of sausage and haddock in her kitchen. Though you vowed to go one better than Woolf: *I will write until I begin to speak my deep self, and then have children, and speak still deeper.*

And that deep self spoke animal truths of which Ted Hughes could only dream. You took enormous creaturely satisfaction in food, in sex, in smells, in your own body and its workings. The smell of your pee first thing in the morning, the texture of your snot when you wiped it beneath a table, the feel of the sun tanning your belly brown and the fine hairs on it blonde, the 'cowlike bliss' of breastfeeding your infant son by starlight. You didn't need any symbolic scaffolding to describe your experience as female animal. Hughes sometimes sounded jealous of animals, for being 'continually in a state of energy which men only have when they've gone mad'. But women have that energy when they're mothering. If he'd observed you a little more closely instead of searching for his next Big Animal Symbol, he might have noticed this, and done justice to the animal with whom he was sharing his bed. I think this is perhaps what drew you to write about the bees you kept in the orchard of your home: their energy – the energy of a hundred parents keeping their brood alive – reminded you of your own.

Here I go again, letting my irritation get in the way of what I should really be saying. I don't think you will mind, Ms Plath – you understood the cathartic uses of a good cleansing female rage. But I must tell you how I lived, and how I died, in order to keep my place in this modern menagerie of animal souls.

I was born into captivity in 1973, a decade after you took your own life. My mother was proud of being one of the original bottlenose dolphins recruited for the US Navy Marine Mammal Program when it was first established. She liked to remind me of my luck at having been born in an elite military training facility. Her point was, I think, that I should be grateful I wasn't born into useless aquarium captivity. This is how she managed her guilt about bringing me into her world, a child who would never know freedom. Is it worse to have freedom and lose it, or not know what it is in the first place? I can't say I've missed it.

Back in 1962, when my mother was in the group of dolphins and California sea lions selected for training, they were kept initially at Point Mugu in California. The Navy trainers quickly realised that the dolphins could be counted on to return to them after being ordered to find or fetch objects, even in open water. The program was expanded and moved to Point Loma in San Diego, and a sister research laboratory was set up in Hawaii. One of the dolphins in the cohort, Tuffy, soon had a breakthrough experience. She successfully carried an important message and supplies down to aquanauts living in the US Navy's experimental habitat, SEALAB II, which had been placed in a canyon off the Californian coast, more than sixty yards underwater.

Tuffy used to keep my mother and the other dolphins entertained by mimicking the conversation between one of the
aquanauts – who was about to emerge from SEALAB II after
spending a world record of thirty days down there – and President
Johnson, who had called to congratulate him. The aquanaut was in
a decompression chamber, and the helium gas had made his voice
high and squeaky. The President gamely pretended not to notice
that he was speaking to someone who sounded like Mickey Mouse.

My mother was always bothered by the stupidity of the Navy's
dolphin-naming policy: why recruit us because of our superior
intelligence then give us dumb names like Tuffy? Her theory was
that the Navy anticipated a public-relations disaster, and hoped that
our goofy names might signal that we were not considered to be
combatants, that we were not so different from Chuck and Loony at
the nearest Sea World. But those in charge had the program classified through the chilliest years of the Cold War, from the late 1960s
to the early 1990s. We could have been given proper combat names
or titles for those decades and the public would have been none the
wiser. Instead, it was my mother's special fate to be called Blinky for
her professional life, and mine to be called Sprout.

My mother's cohort, MK6, was trained to protect assets such as
ships or harbour constructions by alerting human handlers to
the presence of enemy divers in the surrounding water. In 1970
she and four other dolphins in her team were sent to Vietnam on
their first tour of service, to guard a US Army pier in Cam Ranh
Bay. They patrolled the area and warned their handler when sabo-
teurs were detected nearby. Her team was subsequently credited by

some for preventing the pier being blown up, though of course this was disputed. The program has always had more detractors than admirers.

In the stoic tradition of military parents, my mother didn't tell me much about her experience in Vietnam, but I could sense some of what she went through because of certain physical stress points throughout her body. She did say that the most difficult part was being transported there and back in a primitively repurposed Navy vessel. My daughter loved that story, and often asked her grandmother to repeat it. She couldn't believe how old-fashioned the vessel was, how basic the resources. By now, a decade after my own death, I'm sure my daughter is deployed to conflicts around the world within hours' notice, transported in the utmost comfort in some kind of fancy bio-carrier that fits into any type of Navy vehicle: ship, helicopter, aircraft, spacecraft. These technologies are developed faster than humans have time to assimilate what they mean – they outstrip men morally in the end, stunning them into submission, and they drag the rest of the world's species along for the ride.

Once my mother had finished her tour of duty and returned to San Diego from Vietnam, the Navy decided to breed some of the next generation of military dolphins within the facility. To that end, she was allowed to mate with her choice of partner among the males in the bachelor pod. Who my father was is irrelevant, as is usually the case in matrilineal societies. I was raised by my mother and the other females among whom I lived, and by my human trainer, Petty Officer First Class Bloomington. I loved him deeply, and not in a Stockholm syndrome sort of way as my mother sometimes teased. I think she was jealous of our bond. Her generation had been trained by men who were a strange blend of traditional and iconoclastic. Those men were attracted to the safe hierarchies of the military, but they were also caught up in the Zeitgeist that had been developing as post-Second World War certainties gave way to the unpredictable, boundary-pushing conflict with the Soviets. Fantastic rumours circulated about scientific and military advances the Soviets were making with the use of animals: bats that could detect weapons stockpiles; cats inserted with bugging devices; pigeons guiding nuclear warheads.

Whatever purpose the US Navy could imagine for us dolphins, they were convinced the Soviets were ten steps ahead of them. They trained my mother's team firmly, as subordinates. They were not interested in building a relationship with them as individuals, but in what they could get out of them as a group in a utilitarian sense. My mother claimed it was better that way, the trainer–trainee relationship less fraught with emotion and need.

But Officer Bloomington was different. When he started working with me in the late 1970s, he was only twenty-one, skinny, newly graduated from college with a marine sciences degree made possible by his Navy scholarship, and ridiculously proud of his tattoo of a seahorse on the sole of his foot (anywhere else and the enlisters would have given him grief for it). One of his professors at college had briefly worked in the Caribbean laboratory established by John C. Lilly in the '60s to carry out all sorts of bizarre, unconventional research on dolphin–human communication, and he got Officer Bloomington onto Lilly's work. It was far too unorthodox for Officer Bloomington – he knew he would never dare do the kinds of things that Lilly had – but it encouraged him to think of dolphins differently. One of Lilly's experiments, for example, required the researcher to take LSD then climb into an isolation tank with dolphins beneath it in a sea pool, to communicate with them on alternate sound waves. Another involved the researcher living in isolation with a dolphin for months in a laboratory flooded with sixteen inches of seawater.

I think Officer Bloomington suspected Lilly was a bit of a creep – so many of the photographs in Lilly's books featured his female research assistants, who all happened to be gorgeous women with long red nails, happy to give horny dolphins belly scratches or hand jobs. But in the interests of my education he read to me from these books, and from anything else about dolphins he could find, scientific or imagined. He would get secretly stoned and read to me about Johnny Mnemonic, a foul-mouthed cyborg dolphin who's a US Navy veteran and a heroin addict. He organised a screening for the trainee dolphins of the Mike Nichols film *The Day of the Dolphin*, projecting it onto the wall opposite our pens. We found the movie quite funny, though we knew it was intended to be serious, because the dolphins playing the characters Alpha and Beta (who were being trained by some bad guys to blow up the President's yacht) kept saying rude things that only dolphins could understand about the lead human actor in the underwater scenes.

When *The Hitchhiker's Guide to the Galaxy* was published, Officer Bloomington read it to me so many times I can still remember most of Chapter 23 by heart (it's a short chapter):

> It is an important and popular fact that things are not always what they seem. For instance, on the planet Earth, man had always assumed that he was more intelligent than dolphins because he had achieved so much – the wheel, New York, wars and so on – whilst all the dolphins had ever done was

muck about in the water having a good time. But conversely, the dolphins had always believed that they were far more intelligent than man – for precisely the same reasons.

Curiously enough, the dolphins had long known of the impending destruction of the planet Earth and had made many attempts to alert mankind to the danger; but most of their communications were misinterpreted as amusing attempts to punch footballs or whistle for titbits, so they eventually gave up and left the Earth by their own means shortly before the Vogons arrived.

The last ever dolphin message was misinterpreted as a surprisingly sophisticated attempt to do a double-backwards-somersault through a hoop whilst whistling the 'Star Spangled Banner,' but in fact the message was this: *So long and thanks for all the fish.*

That used to crack Officer Bloomington up every time he read it, though it might have had more to do with the quality of his weed. Sometimes, on nights when I couldn't get half of my brain to fall asleep, I would amuse myself thinking up alternate lines for the dolphins' final message to humans, with the restriction that I could only use titles of songs I'd heard being played on the radio at our facility. The line would depend on my mood, and what I'd been asked to do that day. Some days it would be 'Da Ya Think I'm Sexy?' On days when I was feeling sentimental: 'Call Me' or 'We Don't Talk Anymore' or 'Don't Let Me Be Misunderstood'. On bad mood days: 'Tired of Toein' the Line'.

Each morning, Officer Bloomington took me from my home pen at Point Loma out into the training area, laid on a rubber mat in the boat. The first skill he taught me to master was how to wiggle myself overboard once he'd pointed my tail in the right direction; the second was how to get myself back onto the boat unassisted at the end of the session. I quickly learned to retrieve a Frisbee, balancing it on my nose like a regular showoff. Over time, our training sessions became more challenging, geared towards teaching me to identify and locate features on the sea floor that might be useful or dangerous to the Navy, such as dropped equipment or mines buried in sediment.

Officer Bloomington understood from the beginning that I knew exactly what was going on. More than anything, he wanted to earn the moral right to give me commands by demonstrating that he considered me to have a form of consciousness as complex as his own. As our relationship developed, he relied less and less on food-reward training, disliking it because it assumed that my needs were base, and also because of the cruel anti-foraging muzzles that had been standard issue in my mother's day.

It was a partnership, one that I was born into, but still. He liked to say we had a true I/thou relationship, quoting some philosopher or other – that we related as subject to subject, not subject to object, and communicated with our whole beings. In another life, I think he would have used his skills differently, as a scientific researcher who observed and recorded, rather than as a handler who had to elicit certain behaviours from us to keep his job. He figured out long before his contemporaries that we use a combination of high- and low-frequency sounds – clicks, buzzes, creaks, whistles – to convey information and emotion, and he learned to identify the signature whistle of each dolphin under his command, which is our own form of naming.

By the time I was fully trained, the Navy had five marine mammal teams, each with specialist skills. My mother wanted me to join MK6, but I was placed instead in MK7, a dolphin-only team who specialised in finding and tagging mines embedded in the ocean floor. The other two dolphin-only teams, MK4 and MK8, worked on locating floating mines in the water column and mapping out safe underwater passages for troop landings onshore. MK5 comprised sea lions (who have no sonar ability but better underwater directional hearing and low-light vision than we do) briefed with naval equipment recovery. There were a few beluga whales in that team, recruited because they also use sonar but can withstand colder water and dive deeper than we can. We didn't see much of the sea lions or whales except on joint training exercises, when we were all operating under strict rules of engagement. I think this suited those in charge of the program. They preferred us to focus our need for communication on the humans training us, and perhaps didn't like to think of us coming up with secret plans and clever tricks together. It reeked of mutiny.

My first tour of duty was in the Persian Gulf in 1987, during the Iran–Iraq war. My MK7 team was deployed to search the ocean floor for embedded mines for a set radius around the 3rd Fleet Flagship USS *La Salle* in the harbour in Bahrain. MK6 was also deployed, to escort oil tankers from Kuwait through safe waters. It was thrilling to finally be part of a real mission after so many years of training, and I remember feeling closer to Officer Bloomington than ever before. I would use echolocation to scan for mine-like objects and report back to him if I found one, knocking a black buoy beside the boat to confirm a sighting. He would then send me to deposit the anchor of a buoy close to the object to alert other Navy vessels, until the object could be checked and deactivated by a specialist team of divers.

We lost two dolphin team members on that mission, not due to sea mines accidentally detonating (this happens rarely, as we are trained not to disturb them and they are programmed to detonate only when a large metal object passes overhead). The dolphins were machine-gunned to death near the surface by Iranian boat-patrol units who had figured out what we were doing. Some native wild dolphins were also killed this way, though we'd tried to keep them away from the area by acting territorially. Officer Bloomington took this especially hard. He hadn't anticipated it as a consequence and blamed himself for their deaths. He felt that the skilled Navy dolphins at least had a chance of defending themselves, but the native dolphins had been put directly in harm's way. He tried to record their deaths officially so that this could be prevented on future missions, but his superiors blocked him, worried about a public outcry.

Back at the San Diego training facility at the end of this mission, I was given a few years to recover from active service, after which I was allowed to breed. I like to think I didn't make the same mistake as my mother, who had encouraged me to believe I had a better life in the Navy than I ever could out in the wild. I apologised to my daughter so often for bringing her into a world of captivity that she found it ridiculous. As it turned out, she was given a choice. When she was born in 1993, our program was being downsized (or 'right-sized', as the expensive consultants liked to call it) in the aftermath of the Cold War, and many of our team members were being retired or released. The Navy put some of the oldest dolphins up for sale to leisure facilities and parks around the US, but nobody was buying – by then, most aquariums or dolphinariums were doing their own breeding in-house.

One morning in the autumn after my daughter was born, Officer Bloomington took all the dolphins under his authority, including me, my mother and my baby girl, out into the bay and released us without giving a specific task or return command. He explained what was happening, speaking respectfully as he always did, trusting us to understand. He anticipated a long, drawn-out retirement process where federal permits would be needed before any of us could be released into the wild, and he wanted to spare us the fate of being trapped where we were no longer needed, or sold off to some depressing sea life park.

My mother decided to try out life in the deep blue sea again. She was forty-seven by then, the only surviving Vietnam War vet from her team. She and I both knew she didn't have much time left, and I understood that she was really choosing a free death, whereas the other six who decided to join her were choosing a free life. They are the only seven dolphins ever recorded as not having returned to their handler in the history of our program. Officer Bloomington stated the cause as unusual disobedience in his logbook and almost lost his job over it, but he'd stalled for long enough to give the escapees a good chance of not being recaptured.

My daughter knew that morning out in the bay that she was free to go. She watched forlornly as her grandmother swam away, sending reassuring clicks and whistles back to her so that she'd know she was not in distress. But like me, my daughter chose to stay, and when the time came she was assigned to MK7. This made me happy, as I knew Officer Bloomington would look after her as he had me. He'd been there from her first moments in the world, supporting me as I birthed her. He'd camped beside my pen for nights as my due date approached so that he would not miss my labour. In the minutes after she was born, in the middle of the night, I nudged her to the surface and held her there while she learned to breathe, and Officer Bloomington literally jumped up and down beside the pool, yelling and whooping.

He named her Officer, so that she might always have a fitting military title as a first name. He understood the significance of her birth for all of us: the third generation of a female military family. Females have served in the US military for much longer than anybody realises, he liked to remind his colleagues in the '80s, when the gender issue was heating up and most of the men were intransigent. Back then, the Navy Marine Mammal Program was still in full swing, with over a hundred dolphins, many of us female, and a massive operating budget. But the men laughed at him. They didn't like to think of us as male or female; we were just animals.

Soon after my mother had decided to die free, a new dolphin arrived at our base in San Diego. His name was Kostya. He was Russian, part of the Dolphin Division trained at the Soviet Navy's secret base on the Black Sea. They too had run into funding difficulties in the years after the Cold War thawed. Kostya and most of his team were up for sale, and the Soviets were prepared to sell to anyone who could afford the exorbitant price, even if the buyer was the very enemy against whom these dolphins had been trained to work.

Kostya arrived with his female Soviet trainer, Chief Petty Officer Mishin, to be the lead dolphin/handler pair in a new, highly classified training program within our facility. Officer Mishin had skin so pale it seemed to glow, especially when she was beside Officer Bloomington, whose years working under the San Diego sun had turned him a nutshell brown. He surprised me by becoming tongue-tied around her – for so long, he had been a confirmed bachelor, committed to us and nobody else. Sometimes, after a training session, I saw him gazing at the puddles she'd left on the jetty as she wrung sea water out of her hair, as if they might give him a clue to understanding her.

He had been instructed to work closely with her and Kostya to learn their training techniques, but he soon realised that Officer Mishin's approach was as gentle as his own. She teased him about this, told him he was gullible to have believed all the rumours of draconian Iron Curtain methods, and in response he would smile a smile I had never seen on him before, shy and delighted and fearful all at the same time, the smile of a man hopelessly in love and unsure if the feeling could ever be mutual. My daughter and I observed all this with a mix of pity and amusement, secure in the fact that the feeling was not mutual, for we could tell from our scanning that Officer Mishin was left unmoved by Officer Bloomington's attentions. We did not want to share him.

Kostya had been kept in isolation for a period before the sale went through, despite Officer Mishin's protests, and for a while he was moody and aggressive because of his confusion, and only allowed to socialise with the group of bachelor dolphins. Once he was allowed to mingle with the females, Kostya also claimed that most of the rumours we'd heard about the Soviets were untrue – much to our disappointment, he told us he'd never been parachuted from a military plane at great heights into the ocean. He did, however, know how to tell the difference between a Soviet submarine and a foreign submarine, and we decided to believe this was ominous just for the thrill of it.

Yet the Navy superiors were convinced that Officer Mishin was hiding something from them. They insisted that Kostya had skills beyond those she allowed him to demonstrate, that he knew how to set sea mines, that he'd been trained to blow up enemy submarines in an emergency kamikaze move, or that – most sinister of all – he had been part of the Soviet Dolphin Division's Swimmer Nullification Program, trained to attach a device to an enemy diver that could be remotely activated to inject carbon dioxide at high pressure into his bloodstream and force him to the surface, killing him. Officer Mishin vehemently denied this, and said she would have refused to train dolphins to go against their very nature, to be killers, that it would be impossible even if she'd tried. She explained that a dolphin is so sensitive to human distress that it would immediately refuse to repeat any command that caused harm. Officer Bloomington backed her up on this. The powers that be were unconvinced.

Swimmer detection in a conflict situation had traditionally been the remit of MK6, my mother's old team, but now that resources were scarce the higher-ups decided that members of MK7 should add this skill to our repertoire. The way it had always worked in MK6 was for the dolphins to alert their handlers to the presence of a diver or swimmer, whether friendly or hostile, and leave it to the humans to decide how to respond. Those in charge now decreed that a special team should be trained to tag a diver with a locating device. Officers Bloomington and Mishin at first refused to participate in this training mission, but when they realised it would go ahead with or without their support, they felt they could better protect us by participating. Their superiors assured them we would never be asked to perform this task in a conflict situation, that it was only about broadening our skill base.

I was selected to be part of this classified program along with the other dolphins who had served with me in the first Gulf War; at that stage we were the only ones in the facility with real-world combat experience. Kostya was also included in the team. We were sent to a secluded Navy research base on San Clemente Island for training.

As the months passed, something about the setting – the isolation of the island, perhaps, or their shared resistance to the thinking behind the mission – began to change the dynamic between Officers Bloomington and Mishin. She started to show signs of affection for him, and quite suddenly, this affection bloomed into something more powerful. She had fallen in love. She kept her feelings hidden from Officer Bloomington, but Kostya and I picked up on them immediately. Soon the love pheromones they were both emitting drenched the air Kostya and I breathed in with each conscious breath we took, but they each suffered in secret, thinking their love was unrequited.

Kostya and I, however, were unable to keep our jealousy a secret from each other because of our cursed scanning ability. He loved Officer Mishin, I loved Officer Bloomington; we did not want to be displaced in their affections, though we knew it was the right and normal nature of events for a man and woman to fall in love.

We wanted them to be happy, but we also wanted to be the primary cause of their happiness. Kostya and I tried to fall in love ourselves, but it felt too much like an act of compensation, and after a while we gave up trying.

This was the first time I had been away from my daughter for an extended time, and I missed her with an intensity that was overwhelming. Being a mother had taught me to live in the present, most embodied moment, to respond to her most immediate needs and tune out all other wavelengths of thought and anxiety, to *be* with her without thinking of past or future. She had surprised me by being her own complete, discrete self as soon as she was born. I had expected her to have a blank-slate quality, but she was herself, utterly, from her first few seconds in the world: composed, cautious, curious. During our separation for those long months at San Clemente, I thought of her constantly. I have never been lonelier.

Officers Bloomington and Mishin took to going hiking on the island on their days off, and afterwards Officer Bloomington would describe the hinterland to me, guiltily, in too much detail, knowing I was unhappy. They had made it their mission to find a surviving feral goat somewhere in the rocky hills. He told me the story of the goats, brought to the island in the nineteenth century and allowed to roam wild as a food source for passing sailors. Eventually they'd become a pest, and a century after the first pairs were brought to San Clemente, the Navy was authorised to eliminate them. Animal rights activists tried to intervene and some goats were put up for adoption on the mainland, but the Navy was given court approval for their extermination. The goats had the upper hand in the terrain and went into hiding, putting the exterminators through their paces. This war of attrition went on for some time, until there was only one small family of goats left on the island. A lone doe was captured and fitted with a radio collar. When released, she led the shooters to her family. She was nicknamed the Judas goat, for betraying those she loved.

Officers Bloomington and Mishin never did find any surviving goats, but it was on one of their hikes together that they revealed their feelings for each other. By the time the San Clemente training mission ended in 1999 and I was reunited with my daughter in San Diego, I had learned to attach a pinging clamp device the size of a golf ball to a human diver, and Officer Bloomington was, for the first time in his forty-one years on earth, engaged to be married. Kostya was as unimpressed by this as I was.

Theirs was a long engagement. I would sometimes entertain fantasies that they were having second thoughts about getting married, but I could sense their feelings were deepening, becoming more layered, binding them more closely together than any official ceremony could. I tried – and tried – to be happy for them.

Officer Bloomington's fear all along had been that if my elite unit performed well on training missions, it would be irresistible for the Navy to put us to work in a real conflict. This was the way military innovation worked. No matter how crazy a method seemed at first, in the right high-stress situation it could all of a sudden be considered legitimate. In our case, the initial catalyst was the terror attack on USS *Cole* in Yemen in 2000. Our team's resources were doubled and we were put on high alert. The following year we were sent to

Norway to participate in the large-scale NATO maritime warfare exercise, Blue Game. And then 9/11 happened.

Something else significant, for my species, occurred in 2001, though understandably not many Americans took any notice in the midst of their grief. A scientist published the outcome of her breath-taking research which showed that we dolphins respond to our own images in a mirror. Previously, other than humans, only higher primates such as chimpanzees had been shown to pass what scientists call the 'mark test', which indicates an awareness of self, something that human children achieve as toddlers. The dolphins in the study, when marked with temporary ink somewhere on their bodies, went straight to an underwater mirror – signalling they could recognise their own reflection – and examined the mark, proving they could also recognise when their appearance had changed. This study confirmed what Officer Bloomington had known about us all along, that we have a sense of self as sophisticated as any human's.

But it prompted me to remember something, a conversation I'd overheard between Officers Bloomington and Mishin about the persecution complex that afflicts most humans, and made me wonder: Why do *you* feel persecuted by *us*? From the mild feeling of being teased without your consent all the way to the other extreme of the terror of recognition, that we might expose you for what you truly are. What use is a sense of self if all it does is make you feel that self to be constantly under siege?

The shock of the terrorist attacks spurred Officers Bloomington and Mishin to set a date for their wedding. At the ceremony, held beside the pen housing me and my daughter and the one housing Kostya, Officer Bloomington read out a paragraph from the mirror-mark research paper, and thanked us for putting up with humans for the millennia we have co-existed. Officer Mishin gave her new husband a large mirror as a wedding present, knowing that he would want to do the mark test with us as soon as they returned from their honeymoon. She promised to use her own lipstick to mark Kostya. The guests laughed, and – I swear it – Kostya blushed with pleasure.

In 2003 I was deployed to the Persian Gulf for the second time in my life. The entire MK7 team, including my daughter, was transported from San Diego to the Gulf in the well deck aboard USS *Gunston Hall*. Our brief was, as usual, to find underwater mines and booby traps laid in the port of Umm Qasr by Saddam Hussein's forces and mark them by dropping acoustic transponders close by.

Halfway through the journey, Officers Bloomington and Mishin were given orders that the special-ops team Kostya and I were part of was to be authorised to put locating tags on enemy divers in the port, as we had been trained to do in San Clemente. They resisted at first, to no avail – in wartime, the military culture of obeying orders becomes cultish, something by which to live or die. They decided to focus instead on getting us ready to do the job as safely and efficiently as possible. The orders were that we would be released on individual tagging missions, one at a time, and I was chosen to go first.

My daughter and I communed during the rest of the voyage, side by side in our travel pods on the well deck. She knew about my special mission but she wasn't concerned about my safety, mostly because of her excitement over her own first deployment. She couldn't wait to get out into the harbour at Umm Qasr to clean up the seafloor and put to shame the unmanned underwater vehicles installed with technological sonar that the higher-ups had insisted on including in the team. She knew – as did our handlers – that nothing could rival our echolocation abilities in this kind of situation, where the shallow water of the port and the reverberations from clutter on the harbour bed would confuse the machines. Only we could be counted on to distinguish between harmless debris, coral rock and anti-ship mines; only we had the ability to detect the different types of metal in an object. The humans liked to send out a sonar-equipped drone named REMUS to do an initial sweep of the embedded objects on the seafloor, but then it would be up to my daughter to work her magic.

The night before I was to be released into the waters of the harbour for my solitary mission, Officer Bloomington took a long time over my health inspection. This was among the first sets of skills he had taught me as a young trainee, to participate in a routine inspection to ensure my fitness to serve. Many of the days we had spent together had started with him inspecting my teeth, then giving me the signal to relax so that he could take my temperature and a blood sample. I had learned to look forward to the moment when he put the stethoscope beneath my pectoral flipper to check my heart rate. I liked the attentive way he listened, looking at me but not seeing me as he counted and timed my beating heart. But on that night, once he'd registered my heartbeat, he kept the metal disk in place for a long time, no longer listening with medical interest, just listening as if he were trying to commit the thudding pattern to memory.

I was released just before dawn. Intelligence reports showed some kind of attack on Navy harbour assets was imminent, but the details were hazy. Officer Bloomington told me to patrol the waters, to remember what I had been taught about identifying enemy divers, and – should I discover one – to bump into him to attach the locating device to one of his limbs, then get the hell out of there. I believed that the titanium clamp I carried would do no harm, that it was a tracker, nothing more, identical to the ones we'd used during training in San Clemente. I have to believe that Officer Bloomington was similarly unaware, that he had been kept in the dark about the nature of the device.

I wonder sometimes if the man I killed felt the momentary euphoria that human survivors of animal attacks have reported feeling. Ted Hughes was fascinated by this idea, that there is relief, joy even, at giving oneself over to the ancient cycle of predator and prey. He had read accounts of a man attacked by a mountain lion in British Columbia who felt nothing but compelled by the cat's golden eyes; of Tolstoy being mauled by a bear and feeling no pain; of Dr Livingston being seized by a lion and going all dreamy. I find this thought reassuring now. Perhaps, as the device injected carbon dioxide into his bloodstream and he began to spiral up through the dark water column, the man I murdered felt his approaching death as a gift, a return to origins.

Men suicide to consolidate a reputation, women suicide to get one. I may have fuelled the sceptics who say female dolphins should not be taken on by the Navy for training, for the same reason women are not always welcomed into the human armed forces. They say we are sentimental, that we feel things too deeply, we fall to pieces, we let guilt destroy us. But I know that if Kostya had been the first one sent out on the mission, he would have done the same. It has nothing to do with being female, and everything to do with being a dolphin.

Humans might be conscious thinkers; we are conscious breathers. It is very easy to choose to die if every breath is a matter of choice. I am not the first dolphin to suicide, nor will I be the last. We take killing a human very hard. It is as taboo for us as killing our own babies. We recognise in you what your ancients used to recognise in us and understood as sacred a long time ago, when killing a dolphin was punishable by death. You used to think of us as being closer to the divine than any other animal on earth, as being messengers and mediators between you and your gods. You honoured us with Delphinus, our own constellation in the northern sky.

And in return, for thousands of years, when we have found a human drowning, we have held him or her up to the surface of the water as we hold our newborns, waiting for them to take their first breath. We have put our own bodies between you and the lurking shapes of sharks. We have swum very gently with your young, with your impaired. We have greeted you with leaps. You should not have forgotten what your own wise ancestors used to know.

Enough of this death talk. My tale should end with life, and it does, in a sense. Before I was released into the water on my final mission, my scan of Officer Mishin revealed to me that she was pregnant with a baby girl, still unbeknown to herself and her husband.

I haven't yet managed to find your soul out here, Ms Plath, though not for want of looking. There are things about you I would still like to know. Lately I have found myself wondering: After Ted

Hughes abandoned you, did you still love his poetry? 'Who am I?' the mythical creature, the wodwo, asks in one of his poems, and like many men, the wodwo decides, 'I am what I want.' You believed in his genius so fervently when you first fell in love, and all through your remarkable – until it unremarkably fell apart – creative partnership of a marriage. So fervently, in fact, that I began to feel I owed it to you to return to his work, to give it a third chance, to see it through your eyes and hear it through your ears.

I went back to his animal poems and fables for children, and this time I noticed – as much as I wanted to ignore it – that there is something he does with language that makes my brain tingle. A reverse act of scanning, human to dolphin. It happened especially when I was reading my favourite, the one about the moon-whale. I would have liked to read it to my daughter. I imagine you reading it to yours, her little elbows resting against your knee. There is nothing quite like a child's gorgeous listening energy, ravenous for her mother's voice.

PSITTACOPHILE

Soul of Parrot

Died 2006, Lebanon

In her isolation, the parrot was almost a son, a love. He climbed upon her fingers, pecked at her lips, clung to her shawl, and when she rocked her head to and fro like a nurse, the big wings of her cap and the wings of the bird flapped in unison.

Gustave Flaubert, A SIMPLE HEART

It's called being a citizen, not just of the world, but of all time. It's what Flaubert described as being 'brother in God to everything that lives, from the giraffe and the crocodile to man.' It's called being a writer.

Julian Barnes, FLAUBERT'S PARROT

A long time ago, thirty years to be precise, when my owner asked her ex-husband, before he was even her husband, how he felt about their impending nuptials, he said, 'Great. Excited.'

No, no, she insisted, she wanted to know how he *really* felt about getting married.

So then, she told me, he cocked his head, just like I sometimes did when I was about to do something she wouldn't like, and said, 'Before we decided to get married, if I walked past a beautiful woman on the street, I felt a little bit happy.'

'And now, when you pass a beautiful woman?' she prompted.

'And now,' he said, 'I feel a bit sad.'

'Okay. Thank you for that. Now ask me.'

He seemed surprised that she wanted him to reciprocate. That was the trouble with them from the beginning.

'How do you feel about getting married?' he asked dutifully.

'I think you commit to marriage with both eyes open, then you shut one eye for ever after.'

He smiled, lifted the morning paper and disappeared behind its folds.

'I think marriage is going to be similar to being whipped and pickled,' she continued, knowing she was about to overstep lines. 'Like they used to do to mutinying sailors in the old days. Whipped as punishment, then pickled with salt to prevent infection. Wonderfully cruel, terribly kind.'

Her fiancé had already lost himself in the exigencies of current events.

She pushed on. 'I think marriage is probably going to feel like George Shaw's platypus – first one he ever saw, brought back from some expedition or another to Van Diemen's Land. Thought it was a hoax – half a duck sewn to half an otter.'

To her surprise, he'd still been listening. 'So which are you?' he said, letting the paper float down to the kitchen table, its edge sucking up the spilt milk. 'Duck or otter?'

He'd missed the point: that she was neither fully, that marriage would force her to metamorphose so that she was half-duck, half-otter, always partly a stranger to herself. She didn't try to explain. She was pregnant with their daughter then and had discovered that in that state she could get away with bad behaviour.

'Whichever was the bottom half, getting the shit end of the deal,' she said, lifting herself heavily from the chair to wash the breakfast dishes.

If nothing else, you could at least say she'd been perspicacious.

It was a year after she saw the Twin Towers falling that my owner delivered the divorce papers, put her goods in storage and came east. Her initial instinct had been to head for Damascus. She wanted her friends in New York to admire her courage. She wanted her ex-husband to be grudgingly impressed. Her daughter, who had always kept her at arm's length, sarcastically suggested Goa was a more suitable destination for a midlife crisis.

The compromise turned out to be Beirut, where she got a job teaching English at the American School. Disappointing at first because, to her untutored appetites, Lebanon didn't seem to count as the real oriental deal. Would there be any souks? In photographs, Beirut looked to her like a dirtier version of Marseille, more Mediterranean than Middle Eastern.

Four years later, when the Israelis started shelling parts of the city, there was no longer any doubt in her mind: she was living in the Middle East. It seemed like a vindication. Until I started plucking out my own feathers so aggressively I drew blood.

Her job at the American School had come with a furnished apartment and a friendly group of ex-pats fond of rooftop barbeques, and she soon established a routine. She didn't find this depressing, as she had during her last year in New York. Going to the fruit shop on the corner, or putting the trash bags outside the door of her apartment to be collected, it was all an exercise in heightened living. A ride in a Beirut taxi spent mostly on the wrong side of the road would leave her exhilarated. Even placing her used toilet paper in the rubbish bin instead of flushing it was interesting.

She powerwalked among the French speakers along the Corniche in the early morning cool and learned where to buy black-berry juice from a street vendor on the way home. On weekends she lay on the sofa on the balcony drinking Lebanese beer, watching the Filipino maid in the apartment opposite ironing with great care her employer's silk bras and panties. When she was hungry she stood barefoot in front of the open fridge and ate pickles and labne direct from their containers. She bought a hookah and blew rings of apple tobacco smoke at the pigeons outside her bedroom window.

When it came to the past, the selective amnesia of the general population suited her just fine. Their powers of willful overlooking were something to which she aspired. She marvelled at their ability to ignore palm trees stunted by shrapnel, sandbags still stacked on windowsills in abandoned houses, or the large chunk missing from the side of the Holiday Inn. Denial, she thought one evening, pass-ing a dead horse inexplicably decomposing in the shallows on the public beach, is underrated.

She decided, rather irresponsibly, to get a pet. Not a dog or a cat, but something exotic to match her own transformation. The pet shop stocked pig-snouted turtles, Rottweiler puppies, baby crocodiles, squirrels, monkeys with gammy eyes. But the moment she walked into the store, she knew what she wanted. I was sitting on the store-owner's shoulder, grooming the hair around his ear with my beak, strand by strand. She hadn't believed in love at first sight until that moment – it had taken her a while to warm up even to her own child.

'Does the parrot talk?' she asked.

'I've tried to teach it,' he said. 'No luck. But it can squawk.'

She watched me launch into a string of somersaults along the counter-top and offered to buy me on the spot. He was reluctant to sell. He had owned me since my birth many years before, the same year the Syrians re-invaded Lebanon and the long civil war fizzled out. She liked the idea of a peacetime parrot that couldn't speak. She increased her offer. He agreed, and included my cage and perch for the price. In her haste to whisk me away before he changed his mind, she forgot to ask him my name.

'If you are lucky,' he said, as she was leaving the store with a towel draped over my cage, 'he will live for another fifty years. Maybe more.'

She emailed her daughter as soon as she could get to an internet café. Her daughter wrote back immediately: *He sure as hell better not live longer than you.*

She called me Barnes, because she had just finished reading *Flaubert's Parrot* and was a little bit in love with the author, whose photograph took up most of the book's back cover. She didn't yet know the standard pet store joke about parrots: you don't own us, we own you.

Her Googling revealed that she had inadvertently adopted a toddler. As the online exhortations from fellow parrot owners accumulated, her joy became feverish. What delight to be needed so acutely! Her ex-husband had tolerated her neediness but not cultivated it in himself; her daughter had been determined to establish her independence from the moment she learned to walk. But there I was with my feathers scattering the light to create an illusion of brilliant green, my fat tongue, my perfect toes. I, Barnes, who would – if she cared for me attentively – grow to love and depend on her as my parent, partner, mate.

She sat and gazed at me, smiling at the black feathers on my head which looked like a toupée and made me seem oddly formal. My body colouring gave the impression that I was wearing a multi-coloured tuxedo, with green wings, a white tummy and stumpy orange legs. She used to say that whenever I opened one clipped wing, she half expected me to launch into the can-can, or the opening song of a piece of musical theatre.

Her routine began to revolve around me. She created a play area for me in her bedroom, with no more than six toys at any time, rotated daily so that I would get neither overwhelmed nor bored. She gave me corn on the cob, pitted plums and peaches, seeds, lemons, beets, quartered cucumbers, knowing I would eat better if I could hold my food myself, and – as a treat – two peanuts a day. She scrubbed kale leaves to rid them of insecticide and draped them on top of my cage. Each day she cleaned my perch, my play area, my dishes, and washed the floor of my cage with disinfectant.

She changed the water in my bath after every dip, misted my feathers using a spray bottle on particularly hot days, blowdried my feathers on unseasonably chilly evenings. She refused visitors because I found them stressful, and turned down invitations from the ex-pats to come along on weekend roadtrips to various Roman or Crusader ruins around the country, not liking to leave me on my own. She let me perch on her forearm and stroked my back feathers, even when I bit her repeatedly. When I ripped into shreds the pages of every book on her shelf, and flung bits of food onto the walls and floor where they became as intransigent as cement, she forgave me.

In the mornings she left for work reluctantly, hearing me squawking from my cage on the balcony even from the street, but gradually I learned to let her go without a noise. She would return in the early afternoon to find me intently watching the seagulls, trying to communicate with them in ungainly, earnest sounds.

Over many months we became inseparable. I sat on the toilet seat while she brushed her teeth, and hung from her loofah while she was in the shower. Each night she prepared two plates of food and we'd sit on the balcony to eat, her on a chair, me on the table. If she sang while she was making her bed, I made sympathetic noises; if she swore at something on the television, I would screech my support of her position. I learned to open her beer bottles with my beak. I stopped biting.

At about seven in the evening I would get sleepy, then grumpy. I'd whine, grind my beak, droop my eyelids and try to snuggle against her chest until she took me to my cage and put me to bed in my little fleece bird tent hanging from the cage top. It was the only time I would go willingly into captivity. Then I'd sleep for twelve hours straight. In the morning I'd wait for her to wake up and hold me over the garbage can, then I'd let loose the most enormous birdshit you can imagine.

She loved that such simple things gave me delight, a shot of joy – hairy poppies in a vase, sunshine, a full bath run just for me. I would chortle, sing, chirp, crow and coo with the pleasure of proximity to her, and groom her ears, her thin ponytail, the back of her hands, the arms of her sweaters, hoping to be groomed by her in return: feathers ruffled, tummy rubbed, head scratched, pin feathers soothed.

Then she met Marty.

One of the other teachers had persuaded her to come up to the Friday evening rooftop barbeque – she hadn't been for so long – and she decided to take me up there with her, on her shoulder.

Marty had just arrived in Beirut to teach at the American School. He was around the same age as her, had come for the same reasons. 'I knew I could sense another New Yorker sending out distress signals from across the crowded roof,' he said to her after making a joke about avoiding the Midwestern types up there, and the Scandinavians too. 'Like sonar waves emitted by a fellow bat in the darkness,' he said.

'A *bat*! Is that what you think of me?' she said.

That kind of thing, until they couldn't breathe they were laughing so hard.

She and Marty shared meaningful looks when one of the younger teachers arrived with his Lebanese girlfriend. The girl looked young, about nineteen, and had a plastic noseguard taped to her face and a slight swelling around her eyes. She didn't pay much attention to me on my owner's shoulder.

'What happened?' Marty said to the girl after introductions. 'Are you okay?'

The girl smiled and touched the noseguard as if to make sure it was still there. 'Oh, nothing,' she said. 'Just a nose job.'

Her boyfriend grinned at Marty. 'I told her that in America the girls pretend they're sick, or having their appendix out, and disappear for a while. But here, it's a badge of honour.'

My owner cleared her throat and smiled politely at the girl. 'Have you been watching the Olympics?' she asked.

'Yes,' the girl said. 'Today I watched the only Lebanese team that does well at the Olympics. The only one that ever gets gold.'

'Which one is that?' Marty asked.

'The shooting team,' the girl said, and brought her hand to her face to touch the noseguard again.

When my owner and Marty went on a date to the National Museum of Beirut she took me along again. There was a video screening of what looked like large blocks of concrete being set with explosives and carefully blown apart. Inside each block, as the dust settled, an ancient Roman statue was revealed. During the civil war, the museum director had hidden these statues by encasing them in concrete. After the war ended, he wasn't sure if the statues would survive having their casements exploded. But they did. My owner and Marty found this very moving.

Months passed, many of them. My owner spent more and more time with Marty; less and less with me.

One evening they took me out with them after dark, when the day's heat had eased. They shared a hookah at one of the outside tables at a café in Solidere, and watched a Saudi woman eating a Big Mac meal, holding her niqab away from her face with one hand, lifting fry by fry out of sight beneath the material with the other. The motion reminded me of an elephant trunking leaves to its mouth. Her husband and young son were seated beside her in normal clothes.

Oh, Beirut gave my owner and Marty too many reasons to get on the old high horse.

She and Marty knew each other well enough by then to share the same hookah but they kept the plastic cap over the tip, not knowing who'd sucked on it the night before. On the table between them was a bowl of green almonds on ice, and cut watermelon.

'Why did you and your wife divorce?' she asked him, moving a watermelon pip with her forefinger around the table.

'When we were first married, all she wanted to do was change me. Change this, change that. Why aren't you this, why aren't you that,' he said.

I could tell she liked his ironic tone. He had long since outgrown wistfulness.

'Then,' he said, 'fifteen years later, she turns around and says – You're not the man I married!' He laughed. 'She says – I don't know who you are anymore!'

That was when she decided to let Marty spend the night.

My owner was watching Marty sleeping beside her, and I knew she was wishing she had his capacity to fall asleep so easily. For her, there was always some anxiety surrounding that surrender: would

she be able to do it, would she be able to fall asleep without having to try? She said her mind played cruel tricks on her. As soon as
she shut her eyes, her brain took its cue to begin scrolling through
the events of the day, spewing out reams of details and images and
things she could have done better, or not done at all.

She felt abandoned. It was the same kind of loneliness she'd told
me she felt when she swam too far out to sea from the public beach
on the Corniche.

She got up and carried me in my cage out onto the balcony. The
night was still warm. She lay on the sofa on the balcony in the dark
with ice packs beneath her feet, listening to the traffic along the
beachfront and looking at the dregs of starlight. She didn't realise
she'd left my cage door open and her heart swelled with fright for an
instant as she felt the first pincer grip of my toes on her upper arm.
She relaxed as I moved up her arm slowly with my rocking sideways
gait, claw by claw, then rounded her shoulder and inched towards her
neck. Gently – very gently – I took one strand of her long hair in my
beak and tucked it behind her ear.

In the morning, she said to Marty that she couldn't do this, they
should never have done this, it was not why she had come to Beirut.

A year passed.
You should never take it lightly, life in the East.

One afternoon, as I was falling asleep in the crook of her arm, we
heard a deep, distant booming that she would have ignored as thunder had the floor of the apartment not moved beneath her feet.

She couldn't see anything unusual from the balcony, so she turned on the television. Israel had launched its first airstrike.

Her only concern was to find a humidifier to protect my delicate lungs from the smoke and air debris. She put me in my cage, covered it, closed all the windows and ran to a second-hand electronic goods store several blocks away. The humidifier was the size and weight of a small fridge, and men stopped to stare at her on the street as she tried to run with it in her arms. She felt no strain. But it turned out to be useless: the power had been cut.

Four days passed. All the other Americans in the building, including Marty, left Beirut by helicopter for Cyprus. He banged on her door as he passed on the stairwell. When she didn't answer, he assumed she'd already been evacuated.

She and I slept during the day. At night she lit candles and sat beside my cage, ready to stroke me when the windows rattled and the ceiling lamp began to swing. Sometimes we could see a flash as the gunboats in the seaport lobbed shells far overhead, towards the south of the city. With each explosion, I dug my toes into the flesh of her arm until she bled.

A disoriented rooster on the roof of one of the surrounding buildings took to crowing hours before sunrise.

I began to screech for hours on end. I stopped eating, ignored my toys, and bit her to the bone when she tried to take me out of my cage. She watched in despair as I self-mutilated, ripping out my own plumage, plucking myself bare. My feathers accumulated in layers on the floor of my cage.

Eventually she tore herself away from me while I was sleeping and found an internet café where the power was working. Her inbox was black with new messages. Her daughter had written five or six times a day in a rising crescendo of panic. Friends she hadn't heard from in years had written in alarm, offering any form of assistance they could think of, most of it useless. Her ex-husband had emailed for the first time since the divorce, begging her to go to the US embassy to be evacuated. They all said they were sick with worry. They all pleaded with her to come home. She basked in their anxiety, smiled at the computer screen.

She couldn't have known, on the day she took one of the last boat jets to Cyprus, that there would be a ceasefire within a month. That morning, she carried my cage onto the balcony and went back inside, trying to pretend she wasn't packing. I knew what she was doing: wrapping the few shrunken apples and pieces of broccoli she'd hoarded in wax paper, filling a water bottle with leftover seeds, putting my favourite toys into a plastic bag.

Out on the balcony, she found me staring at the sky, my eyelids drooping. I didn't make a sound when she threw a towel over my cage in a furtive movement. She dragged her suitcase with one hand, clutched my cage with the other, and made her way slowly to the pet shop many blocks away. It was dark inside, locked up, display windows emptied. There was no sign of my first owner.

What choice did she have but to hook my cage to the awning overhead and leave as quietly as she could, before I realised I was alone?

Acknowledgements

Thanks first and foremost to Teresa Dovey for her beautiful illustrations. Heartfelt thanks to Sarah Chalfant and Charles Buchan for their unwavering support over many years (and for not reporting me to the madhouse when I sent them a manuscript filled with talking animals). Special thanks to Margaret Stead for welcoming me back to Atlantic Books, and to Sam Redman for her belief in this book. Thanks also to Will Atkinson and Karen Duffy at Atlantic. Thanks to Boria Sax for first sparking my interest in animals in folklore (and for inspiring the book's title). Thanks to Michelle de Kretser, Anna Funder, Jessica Berenbeim, Alex Massouras, Hisham Matar, Diana Matar, Owen Sheers, Nam Le, Nadia Davids and Joanna Jeffery for encouragement along the way. Thanks to Lindiwe Dovey, Robert Mayes, Chiara Dovey-Mayes, Ken Dovey, Teresa Dovey, Blake Munting and Gethin Dovey-Munting for constant support and love.

A much earlier version of 'Red Peter's Little Lady' was published in *Canteen*, Issue 5 (2009), and of 'Psittacophile' in *To Hell With Journals B: East & West* (2007).

A note on sources

Given that these stories pay homage to many authors who have written about animals, I am indebted both directly and indirectly to multiple works of literature. Many of the animal narrators intentionally use words, phrases and sentences taken verbatim from the work of other authors. A complete list of these sources can be found at ceridwendovey.com. Grateful acknowledgement is made for permission to reproduce the extract from *The Hitchhiker's Guide to the Galaxy*, by Douglas Adams, © 1979, reprinted by kind permission of the Estate of Douglas Adams.